The Vanished Mage

Also by Penelope Hill from Elsewhen Press

Working Weekend

The Vanished Mage

Penelope Hill and J.A. Mortimore

Elsewhen Press

The Vanished Mage
First published in Great Britain by Elsewhen Press, 2022
An imprint of Alnpete Limited

Elsewhen Press, PO Box 757, Dartford, Kent DA2 7TQ
www.elsewhen.press

British Library Cataloguing in Publication Data.
A catalogue record for this book is available from the British Library.

ISBN 978-1-915304-08-7 Print edition
ISBN 978-1-915304-18-6 eBook edition

Designed and formatted by Elsewhen Press

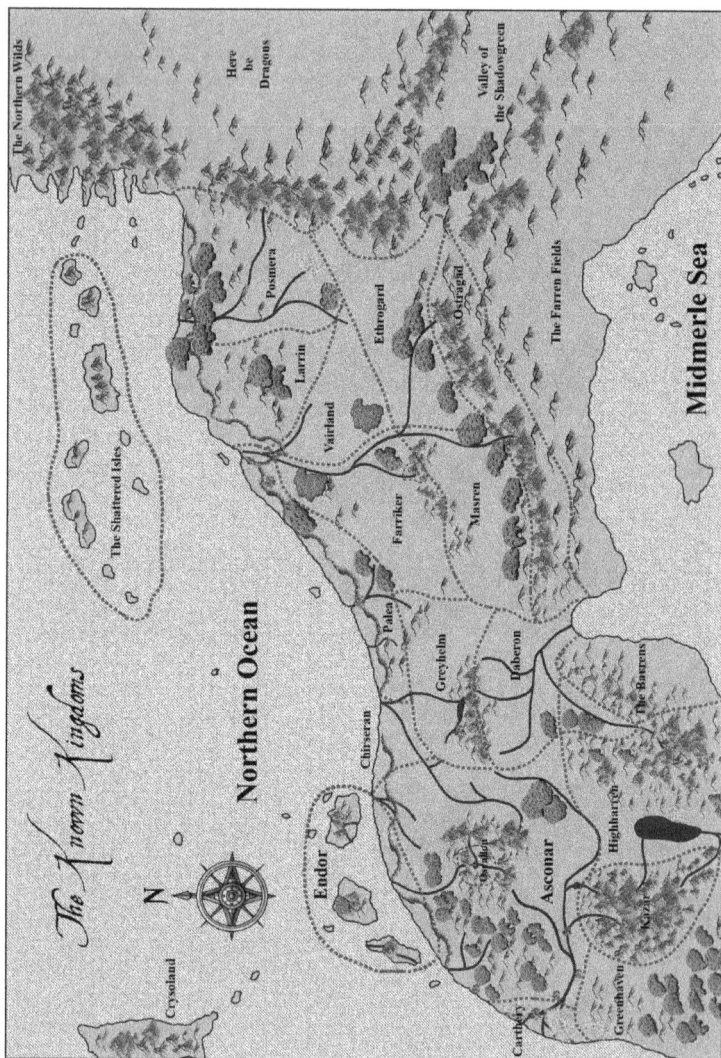

The Known Kingdoms

The Northern Wilds

Here be Dragons

Valley of the Shadowgreen

The Shattered Isles

Posmera

Larrin

Ethrogard

Ostragird

The Farren Fields

Vairland

Masren

Farriker

Midmerle Sea

Northern Ocean

N

Palen

Greyhelm

Haberon

Chitveran

The Bastrens

Endor

Gradun

Ascornar

Highharrgör

Kozarr

Cryoland

Greenhaven

Carthen

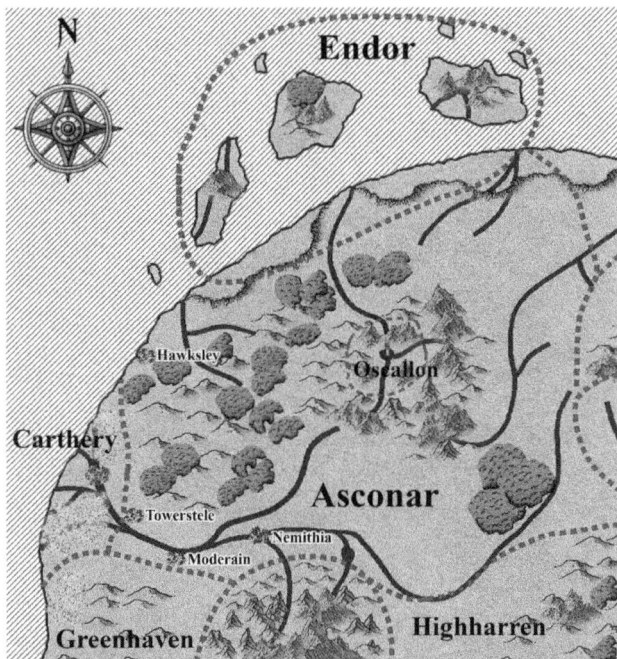

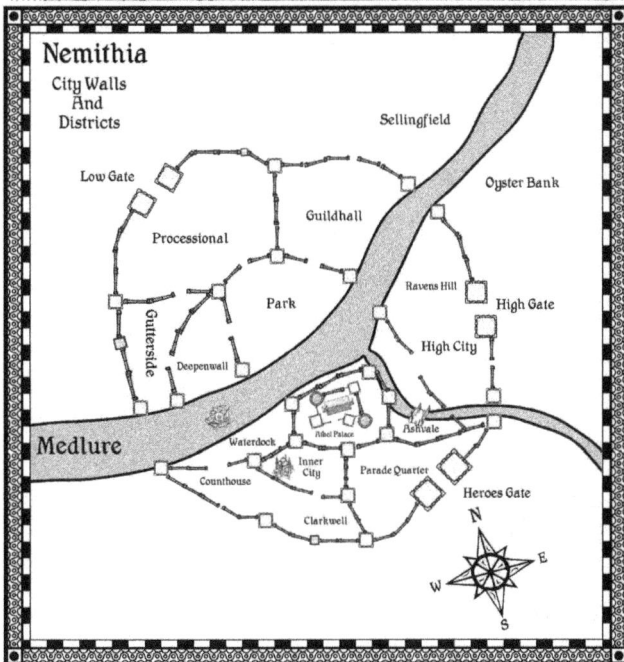

Prologue

Archmagus Reinwald was walking among the stars. The subtle music of the spheres surrounded him, crystal susurrations spun from a thousand sources serenading his every step. His feet left no mark in the darkness of the void as he paced among the constellations. The hem of his robe brushed through planetary rings, and its colours flared briefly as a comet dived unheeded into its folds. He paused before the slow tumble of an azure world, frowning as he considered the pattern its twin moons traced around it, one hand stroking thoughtfully at his beard while the other reached out to plunge through the coral red surface of the larger sphere and leave ripples of disturbance in its patterned surface.

The starlit frown deepened across his cragged face. He stepped sideways to consider the movement from another viewpoint, seemingly unconcerned as he was slowly engulfed by the stately progress of the blue spun world at his back. Just as slowly, his figure re-emerged from the swirl of cloud and continents while the planet tumbled on, its surface eddied with the marks of his passage.

Somewhere in the endless darkness that was eternity a door opened, spilling the flickering light of a candle flame into the stellar deeps. Reinwald looked up with irritation, his frown deepening into disquiet as he recognised the silhouette of the intruder.

"How dare you," the mage declared, his voice echoing across the vastness that lay between them. "You know that I do not wish to be disturbed. Begone. We will speak later."

The figure behind the candle shook its head. "No, master," the voice said softly. "The time for your words is past. I will not hear them again, this night or any other."

Starlight glinted in the old man's eyes as they narrowed

to consider the speaker. "You are leaving?" he hazarded, a hint of relief in the suggestion. "Has your impatience grown strong enough to risk your contract with me?"

"You have not kept your bargain," the intruder snarled. "You said you would teach me all you know, and yet all you offer me is dry and dusty words."

Reinwald snorted his disgust at the accusation. "You do not have the patience to master the Art," he said. "Nor do you understand what I have taught you. You desire power without the will to pay for it. All you will ever know is a few parlour tricks to impress the ignorant. Go if you wish; I have no desire to keep you. I will bestow my mastery on one who is capable of encompassing it."

"Keep it for yourself," the shadow laughed softly. "I have already taken most of what I am due. Have no concern for me. You will never be disturbed in here again."

Puzzlement and anger flittered over the starlit features of the mage, only to be replaced by sudden alarm. His hand lifted in a warding gesture – too late to stop the confident pronunciation of a single word.

Chapter One

I was immersed in my second attempt to read Duke Bayferry's treatise on the use of winged cavalry when the herald arrived. It was a damp autumn morning, the kind that found all but the most dutiful cloistered within dry walls. Delph – my squire – and I had attended the processional gathering in the Inner City earlier that day, visiting both Our Father's sanctuary and Our Lady's Chapel in the early hours after a night of vigil and prayer, so I had no intention of making any more forays into the drizzled streets. My friend, of course, had risen late and gone no further than the window before deciding to remain at home. By the time our unexpected visitor appeared Foo was firmly ensconced before the fire, studiously intent on being as lazy as possible.

The Inner City clock had just struck the eleventh watch when Delph knocked hesitantly at the chamber door. I looked up as he entered – with some relief, I have to say, since Bayferry's ramblings were tedious and left me wondering whether he'd ever seen a war eagle, let alone ridden one. The intermittent thunk of Foo's throwing knives embedding themselves into the mantelpiece was proving equally irritating, and the interruption was a welcome one.

"My pardon, my lady," Delph began, "but there is a Lord Jarman below, asking for you."

I laid the Duke's treatise carefully on the table before favouring my anxious squire with my full attention. He was growing into a promising young man, although it would still be some time before he was ready to leave my service and start to earn his knighthood. "Very well. Take his cloak to dry at your fire and show him up, will you? Then fetch us a flagon of spiced wine. Garrick will have set one to mull when he saw the weather this morning."

"Yes, my lady." The young man bobbed his head and went, leaving Foo to roll onto his stomach and flick his ears forward with interest.

"Now, what would send an apprentice herald to our door on such an unpleasant day?" he wondered. I shrugged, marking my place in the treatise with a slip of linen before reaching to place the neatly written papers back into their carved box.

"The Master Herald, perhaps?"

His whiskers twitched as his lips curled into what I knew to be a smile despite the fearsome array of teeth it revealed. "Hah," he said and stretched, a movement that reached from finger to tail tip. The tardy note of the palace clock rang out as he did so, obscuring the sound of footsteps on the stairs, but Foo sprang easily to his feet and was decorously perched on the window seat by the time the door opened for the second time.

Lord Jarman was a gangly youth of, at first glance, no more than fourteen summers, wearing the formal red/gold herald's tabard over a courtly tunic and white silk hose. Everything looked a size too large for him with the exception of his hose, which were laced so tightly his legs looked like a pair of spindled sticks thrust into his muddied boots. His hose was spotted with the same mud, suggesting a hurried gait, although whether that was because of weather or because he'd been in haste to reach us was difficult to judge. The bottom of the tabard was dark with damp and his cheeks had been scoured red by the wind.

He dangled his herald's baton of office by its scarlet straps, its burnished gold length wrapped with the white bands of his apprenticeship. Only two remained, showing how close he was to becoming a journeyman in his craft. His left hand rested anxiously on the sword hilt at his side; a gaudy piece designed more for show than practicality. He was clearly never destined to be much of a warrior, but then heralds are not expected to be skilled in arms and rarely prove themselves to be so. There was a wary look on his face as he stepped into the room.

Most of the younger group at court are afraid of me, even if I try hard not to reinforce their apprehensions.

His eyes flicked quickly around the chamber, perhaps a little surprised at its simplicity. I do not choose to live in the over-stuffed splendour that can be found among many of the Asconar nobility, and restrict my love of colour to the subtle tapestries with which I line my walls. My furniture is plain and un-gilded, and even my windows are of clear, not patterned, glass. The thick fur rug at the hearth is Foo's, of course. He has a much greater love of luxury than I.

"My lady," Jarman greeted me, executing a courtly bow which betrayed hours of practice.

"Lord Jarman," I acknowledged in return, rising to my feet in courtesy and responding with the noncommittal dip of my head that I use on all but the most formal of occasions. "Do you bear a message for me, or is this a personal visit?"

He hesitated briefly, glancing at Foo's seemingly casual perch by the window. "Well – ah ... I bear a message, but this isn't exactly official."

I said nothing but gestured him in, keeping the threatened smile from my eyes as I did so. My reputation for soberness has served me well for many years and the mask has become a habit I do not break with ease. He scuttled across to stand close to the fire and lifted his wand of office to fiddle with it distractedly. "The truth is," he said, "that now I'm here it seems a somewhat foolish errand and I hesitate to disturb you with it. But I am sent by Royal command, and so I really should discharge my duty..."

I sank back into my chair and eyed him thoughtfully. "Who has commanded you to me, Lord Jarman? The King? Queen Sharasaan?"

He shook his head, tightening his grip on the painted baton and trying to set his shoulders a little straighter. "His Royal Highness, Prince Broderick, my lady."

Foo's mouth curled open in a silent laugh and his tail quivered with sudden amusement. Had we been alone I might have admonished his reaction to the name, however much I might sympathise with it. Broderick, youngest son of my lord Alwick, is the most beloved of all of Asconar's princes, and that includes the devotion of his elder brothers. Everybody adores him, and a simple request from his lips will suffice to send the most craven of the court into danger without a second thought. Fortunately he has proved worthy of such loyalty, being both kind and noble to the soul. He will serve both his country and his king well in the years to come. It was small wonder that Jarman had agreed to brave the terrors of my sanctum if Broderick had made him come. I wondered if he would have proved so bold if the Master Herald had been behind the order, then dismissed the thought as unworthy of me. A herald always bears his messages, no matter what the price. They give their word to do so.

"Such commands cannot go unheeded," I told him diplomatically. The tension in his stance melted a little.

"No, my lady."

"Then speak your message and have no fear I will judge you foolish for bearing it."

Jarman nodded and shifted into the formal stance he had been taught to adopt: feet slightly apart, his shoulders back and one hand on each end of the gilded baton. He took a deep breath and held for a silent count of five before he began.

"From Broderick, Prince of Asconar, Earl of Carlshore and Thorn, Duke of Wicksborough, Baron of Highbury and Warden of Dershanmoor, to My Lady Parisan, King's Investigator, greetings."

The young man's voice was steady and assured, well versed in the art of delivering a message verbatim without comment or interpretation. As he spoke I made a mental note to commend his presentation to Lithian, the Master Herald, next time we met.

"It has been brought to my attention that a certain Reinwald, Master Historian, noted Archmagus and tutor to our court in this city of Nemithia, has this day failed to report to the duties awaiting him. I do ask you, as my

6

father's most loyal servant, to seek the cause of this laxity and bring word of the mage to me, so that my concerns as to his safety be allayed."

Safely at the end of his recitation the messenger relaxed; enough at least to let a somewhat anxious smile tug at his expression. I suspected he was relieved to have found himself word perfect. I also wondered how long Broderick had laboured to phrase that formal a missive, thus betraying both his youth and his uncertainty of me. Alwick's heralds bring terser words, and they aren't usually so polite.

Foo's tail was a positive rumble of laughter and he shot out his hand to pin the betraying quiver under a sudden pretence of casual grooming. Jarman caught the movement but I doubted he understood the reason for it. There are very few humans who can read a R'rruthren as well as I, and that is only through long acquaintance and the occasional misunderstanding. My companion's amusement was probably well founded, if a little impolite; I am one of Alwick's many hands and can be sent to soothe, to protect, to enforce, and even to avenge if I am so commanded. Many, both in Asconar and elsewhere in the Known Kingdoms, have sought my aid, for I am sworn to help those who petition me with true need. I have thwarted plotters, dispelled enchantments, fought demons, and even laid the dead to rest; it would not seem to be my task simply to enquire of a prince's tutor why he might be late to his lessons. Not on first examination, at least.

All the same…

I have learned to trust my inner voices. My dedication drives me in ways that few can understand and fewer still would choose if they did, but I have never been called upon without reason, however unlikely the paths I have had to walk. There was nothing in this uncertain youth and his carefully phrased request to suggest anything more than a princely prank devised to occupy a damp day; nothing, perhaps, except that Broderick was his father's son and well aware of my particular skills.

Curiosity tugged at me, pushed a little, perhaps, by boredom, but roused by something deeper; my hand went to the crystal at my throat and it flared beneath my touch, a silence of white light that spoke louder than words.

Jarman's eyes went wide and he stepped back in alarm. Over by the window Foo abandoned his tail and stared at me instead. "By the Hunter," he growled in some astonishment, "are you saying *yes*?"

***

"Master Reinwald comes to the palace twice a week to lecture us in history," Jarman explained between careful sips of the mulled wine that Delph had brought him. His hand was still shaking slightly – from reaction, not cold, since he'd had plenty of time to warm himself by our fire.

"Us?" Foo enquired, loping across to the table where my protégé was filling two further goblets with Garrick's spiced brew.

Our messenger nodded, pausing to breathe around the sudden warmth that had flooded his throat.

"Those in my cohort," he explained. "There are three more of my ranking apprenticed under Master Lithian, and then there is the prince, and some of the squires, and others desirous of study. The Archmagus will not take anyone into his class until he thinks them old enough to take him seriously. He's very meticulous and insists on everyone being exactly on time and totally attentive. He hands out the strictest punishments for tardiness – even to the Prince. When Gyneth missed an entire lesson because of her hawk, he made her learn all of the clauses in the fourth Endorian Treaty. One for every minute of his wasted time, he said."

Foo's whiskers twitched at the thought. I nodded in sympathy, remembering the days of my own lessons and equally insistent tutors. "So the Magus is never late to your lessons himself?" I hazarded.

"Never. He always sends word if he cannot come – along with work to do in his absence – but that isn't often. He's in the study hall by the third strike of the ninth watch and we must be in our places by the time the last bell is sounded."

The information confirmed my suspicions. I knew a little of Reinwald's reputation, even though I was barely acquainted with the man himself. On the rare occasions I had seen him at court, his punctiliousness had incurred comment. "Were you on time today?"

Jarman nodded, cradling the warm wine against his chest. "Every one of us. Except the Archmagus. There was no sign of him, and no word, either. After a while the prince sent servants down to enquire at the gates, but no-one had seen him. We waited nearly a watch out before we realised he wasn't coming at all."

"If Broderick –" I caught back my tongue and corrected my informality with barely a hesitation, "– His Highness could send servants to enquire of the palace guard at the gates, why did he not just send them further, into the High City, to ask of Reinwald himself?"

Foo's expression affirmed my question. It would have been the obvious step to take. The messenger coloured visibly and drank deeply to cover his reaction; a mistake, since Garrick's concoctions are not particularly subtle, just effective. He coughed and spluttered for a moment before he regained his breath. "His Highness thought … that is, we didn't suppose … it was Gavin's suggestion …" He tailed off and stared down into his goblet with a notably guilty look. Whatever they had done, it was obviously something they shouldn't have. The confession had to be made, however, and after a moment he looked up and met my eyes. "The Archmagus uses an imaging glass," he began hesitantly. "He set it up in the study hall to show us the sites of battles and some of other places he has visited. We had strict instructions not to touch it, and none of us have, except … Fabian said he understood the commands the Master used – he's studying sorcery and enchantment with Lord Augis so knows the importance of pronunciation – and Gavin dared him to try it, and

Broderick ordered him and Tess said she'd act as focus ..." Broderick, not 'His Highness', nor 'the prince'; Jarman had dropped the handicap of formality and was telling it to me as it had truly happened. I could picture the situation with ease: the young prince, bored with waiting for an old man who had never failed him before, tempted to a challenge he could not resist – the chance to play, unsupervised, with the toys of those much wiser than himself. Magic is not a thing to unleash lightly, and it was clear that Jarman, at least, had learned that lesson well.

"All we wanted to do was find out why the Archmagus was so late. Fabian said the glass would locate its master easily – the easiest thing to do with it, he thought. Tess looked into the mirror and then he said the words – Fabian, that is – and the whole thing misted over, the way it should do ..." The young voice became hesitant, confessing to something he had not found to his liking at all. "There were ... stars, after that. Stars and a shadow in the darkness. It looked like – it moved like a man – and," he swallowed hard at the recollection, "it called Fabian by name."

Foo's ears flicked forward at this revelation, the goblet suddenly forgotten in his hand. "Was it Reinwald?" he asked.

Jarman had paused for another gulp of the wine; he looked up at the question and shuddered.

"I don't know. It was distorted and sounded as if it came from a great distance. Tess screamed, and Fabian started making gestures of warding, and then the glass cracked. Right across. With a sort of quiet shriek. After that it was just a mirror."

Just a mirror: an instrument of magic shattered by forces its innocent users could not control, and a chance to locate its owner lost because of youthful bravado. The incident had clearly been unnerving, and was layering confusion over a simple mystery – sufficient perhaps to make Broderick consider consulting me rather than taking a simpler course of enquiry.

"It spoke his name," I mused, identifying that as part of the puzzle. An absent mage was no obvious cause for concern, but a magic mirror that identified its unauthorised user certainly was: concern at least for the guilty party.

Jarman nodded. "It called him. Fabian, Fabian. Then a jumble of words – 'say no there', or something like that, and then theory – at least," he added, doubtfully, "that's what we thought, only it happened so quickly and Tess was screaming over the last part, so I can't be sure."

"Another tongue?" Foo suggested. The youth looked at him in surprise.

"Of course," he realised. "Why didn't we think of that? It sounded like it should mean something, but then it would – wouldn't it? Only we wouldn't understand if it wasn't in Gespian, I suppose."

I fought back another threatened smile and considered my visitor carefully instead. "How many tongues have you been taught, Apprentice Herald?"

"Six," he answered promptly, then grimaced. "That is," he admitted, "I am learning six, in addition to my own. I'm good at Dethick, though."

"So's every merchant on the street," Foo growled under his breath. I pretended not to hear him.

"But you didn't recognise these words as making sense in the traders' tongue?"

"No. I don't think so. Is it important?"

"It might be." I sighed and swirled the last of the wine in my goblet as I considered what I had heard. "No matter. It may be nothing at all. Go back to His Highness. I will go to Reinwald's dwelling and ask word of him. This time," I added warningly. The journey might turn out to be no more than a flitter chase and I would not like to encourage Broderick in thinking of me as just another palace flunky, always at his beck and call.

"Thank you, my lady." Jarman bowed deeply and left, relief written over every inch of him.

"I'd say you were a fool, but I know better." Foo bounded back to the hearth to retrieve the knife he had left quivering in the mantleshelf. "There are three things best left undisturbed in this world: the sleep of the dead, the coffers of a Daberon prince – and the business of mages."

I laughed softly, moving towards the inner stairway and the upper floors beyond. "You left out the lazing of a R'rruthren. You don't have to brave the weather. I said I would go. I have nothing to fear from Archmagus Reinwald – although I don't know what he will say when he hears his imaging mirror has been broken."

I left him thinking of a suitable riposte while I climbed to my chamber and slipped into the rest of my armoured finery. By the time I came down again he was standing at the top of the outer stairway with his cloak round his shoulders and mine over his arm. I took it from him without a word, but his whiskers twitched and he shrugged his shoulders with dismissive nonchalance. "I need some air," he explained. "It's not good for a hunter to spend all his time cooped up inside stone walls."

"No," I agreed, opening the door and waving him ahead of me. "Not good for him at all."

Chapter Two

Reinwald lived in one of the many small mansions that can be found nestling on the slope of Raven's Hill, in the southwest of the High City. We walked down Palace Parade and through Ashvale to reach it, the paved streets slicked with rain and populated only by scurrying figures intent on their own business. I asked directions of the duty warder at Medrick's Gate and he sent us up the Raven Steps and into the maze of quiet streets where vulgar commerce is not allowed to disturb the peace of the wealthy.

The Archmagus owned one of the more modern houses that had been built on the hillside, a sturdy half-timbered place that had probably replaced an earlier stone mansion. It was the size of a prosperous inn, boasting its own courtyard and a sizeable garden, all walled off from the street by an imposing brick wall twice the height of a man. Within its grounds the house squatted like a clump of black and white mushrooms. The roof of the main building sported angled peaks and slopes that hinted at converted attics and latter additions, one end standing higher than the other. At the front, the upper storeys jutted out in a series of overhanging steps above the brick-built lower floor. At the back, a squat square tower stuck out of the roof, looking like a left-over remnant of the previous structure. It barely reached above the tiled ridges, forcing the chimneys to crowd together on either side. The whole property sat at a junction of paved avenues, occupying an isolated island amid the slow eddies of stone and brick that swirled across the slopes: one more anonymous building among the discrete streets of Raven's Hill.

Foo and I paced around the outer wall before disturbing the peace of the place. There was a small gate at the rear that led into the sheltered garden. It was locked, but through it we could see a well-tended patch of green complete with fruit trees and spiralling pathways. The back wall of the house supported an outer stairway, which led up to a balcony on the third floor, pausing at the second to include entry at that level. Foo peered through the wrought gate and snarled in quiet approval. One of the main reasons we had chosen our tower in Kellmarch House had been the access to its secluded inner garden. This was more exposed, since the wall was separate to rather than being part of the outer wall of the house, but all the same it offered generous privacy.

At the front, the wall was pierced by a curved archway and another ornate wrought iron gate. This one was open, latched back to allow entry to the courtyard beyond, and the arch was large enough to accommodate a small carriage. The house sat at the back of a cobbled square, which was flanked by brick-built stables on one side and a whitewashed servants' hall and kitchen on the other. Everything seemed to be shut up tight against the penetrating mizzle that had slicked the cobbles and left pools of water around the iron-gridded drain in the corner by the wall, but someone was whistling cheerfully from inside the stable and a small watch griffin scrabbled out of a shelter by the gate and growled at us as we stepped under the arch. Foo growled back, which made the griffin back away shaking its wings in alarm, and I relaxed, stilling my instinctive reach for my sword. This was clearly the right house. Few, even among the nobles of Nemithia, can afford the luxury of a griffin guard, but I had heard that Reinwald was well travelled – he had probably caught and trained this one himself.

The beast's alert brought a man out of the stable door, and he shooed it back into its shelter with a casual wave of his hand. The creature was chained, I noted, although by a length long enough to allow a modicum of flight should it feel the need to stretch its wings. It probably perched on the outer wall in good weather, an effective deterrent to hawkers and a discouragement to the unwelcome visitor.

The man had a weather-beaten face and walked like a warrior despite the lack of weapons at his belt. He wore a leather apron and had been carrying a hay fork, which he'd dropped against the stable wall as soon as he saw us. He wiped his left hand against the apron and hurried over to greet us, pulling his floppy leather hat down against the rain as he did so. He blinked a little as he registered the face of a R'rruthren inside the hood of Foo's cloak but recovered quickly, offering a careful bow while he eyed us up and down. The elaborate weave of Foo's cloak and the fact that the fur trim on mine showed no sign of damp must have convinced him we were worth attention: he bowed a second time, much deeper than the first, and waved us ahead of him toward the house. Both our cloaks were gifts from a grateful True Weaver in Greenhaven we once helped; the enchanter had bespelled them against the weather, and they provide a little more protection against a cold wind than does ordinary cloth. Foo had chosen a dark swirl of green and purple to pattern the intricate fabric, and its velvet texture screams discrete wealth with every drape. Mine is a simple white, trimmed with snowsnake fur and tiny bells that mask the sound of my armour when I walk, and its hood is spacious enough to swallow my helm with ease.

The man ushered us into the porch of the main house and pulled at the handle beside the door. A quiet chime of bells answered the gesture and within moments the heavy oak door was swung wide, revealing a middle-aged woman in a dark kirtle and woven over-robe, a jangle of keys dangling from her belt. I knew Reinwald to be a bachelor; this had to be his housekeeper. "Yes?" she asked courteously.

Foo tipped back his hood and bobbed her a brief bow. "The Lady Parisan to see the Archmagus," he announced.

The woman's face fell. "Oh," she said, and glanced at the man who still hovered behind us. "I see. Well, you'd better come in. Thank you, Eachan, you may return to your work." The man bowed again and scurried away into the rain, leaving us to step into the spacious hall and

15

take in the wide sweep of stairs that dominated it. "If you will let me hang your cloaks," the woman said warily, "I will escort you upstairs. I don't know if the Master will see you, though. He left orders three days ago he was not to be disturbed, and I haven't seen him since."

Foo threw me a sideways look, twitching one ear round towards me as he did so. I knew that to be the R'rruthren equivalent of raising both eyebrows with significance, but the woman gave him a nervous glance. "Is that usual?" he enquired.

"Oh yes." She took his cloak and then offered her arm for mine. I drew it off carefully and she looked a little taken aback by the gleam of armour that lay beneath it. "The Master often works long hours," she explained, moving to hang the cloaks in a nearby alcove, "and sometimes his endeavours can occupy several days. It's odd, though," she added as she led us up the first flight of the sweeping staircase. "He always lets me know if his work will overstep his other commitments, and he was supposed to be teaching today. I don't think he said anything to the lads, either."

"The lads?" Foo is always quicker with the casual questions than I am, which is probably just as well: many people find me intimidating, and tend to respond more easily to his disarming chatter. The housekeeper was no exception; she coloured a little behind the fond smile his query induced.

"The Master's apprentices. This is their floor," she added as we reached the first landing. "They work and sleep up here. Nobody goes above this level without the Master's permission." She drew to a halt beside a small gong that hung discretely at the foot of the next flight of stairs. "He wards it, you see. Nothing serious if you have to go up, but it makes your ears buzz for hours afterwards."

Foo's nose twitched in wary anticipation. Although few of his race carry an aptitude for serious magecraft, many of them are sensitive to the use of power in its various forms. Active magic makes Foo sneeze, a reaction which has proved both a blessing and a curse over the years.

The gong rang with a soft but penetrating note. The woman struck it twice in quick succession, then a third time after a short count. "This warns him of visitors," she said, gazing up the staircase in expectation. After a moment she shook her head: whatever she had been waiting for had clearly not come. "I'm sorry," she murmured, turning to me with an apologetic smile. "He must be too busy to be disturbed. Perhaps you should come back tomorrow."

I considered it. The lack of apparent concern in the Archmagus' household did not support Jarman's sense of unease at his teacher's absence. Foo obviously thought our mission had proved to be a flitter chase after all and turned to make his way back along the landing and down the stairs. At that moment a loud explosion echoed from further into the first floor, rattling the entire building. The woman grabbed at the gong as it swayed on its stand and Foo leapt backwards in alarm, landing easily on a higher step with a throwing knife in either hand. My own hand had flown to my sword hilt, but I did not draw the blade; nothing followed the ominous rattle but a faint indication of smoke from down the corridor, and our escort did not seem to be unduly disturbed.

"Young Master Deckle cannot get that spell right," she sighed. "The Master will not be pleased. Will you excuse me? I must make sure they are in one piece in there."

"Of course." I let her bustle away and turned to share a wry look with Foo. If there is one thing more dangerous than an experimenting mage, it is an apprentice mage experimenting. He was sheathing his knives with a resigned sigh.

"So much for not disturbing the 'Master'," he said, glancing at the landing above him as he did so. "That bang was almost loud enough to waken the dead." He leant against the banister and extruded a single claw with which to scratch at an itch under his left ear. "With any luck the Archmagus himself will come hurtling down here any minute and you and I can get back to our fire."

I nodded abstractedly. There was something wrong with the situation and I was having difficulty putting my finger on it. He was probably right; Reinwald would undoubtedly appear in search of the unfortunate apprentice and then... The reason for my unease suddenly clicked into place and I stared up at the higher landing with growing disquiet. "Foo," I requested slowly, "go up a little further, would you?"

He looked a little surprised but did as I asked, bounding upwards with a lithe step. He was nearly at the top before he also realised what should have happened and hadn't. "Hunter's breath," he swore, "I thought these stairs were warded!"

"So did I." I followed him upwards, my shoulders tensing in expectation of magical assault. Nothing attacked me, or even unsettled me. The staircase was completely free of any protection whatsoever, and Foo's nose had not twitched once beyond that initial anticipation. If Reinwald had set magical wards they were either so subtle as to be unnoticeable or they were no longer in operation.

"Something around here smells fishy," Foo remarked as I joined him.

"Almost undoubtedly," I replied. His lips curled up, revealing a set of gleaming teeth while his tail quivered and his ears flicked in silent laughter. I looked at him in some surprise. "Something I said?"

He shook his head and might have been about to explain, but the woman chose that moment to return. She reappeared on the landing with a young man of seventeen or eighteen in tow, a youth so obviously born to be a mage it might have been written on him in words of white fire. He was tall and lanky, with short straggly hair and a head as narrow as the rest of him, his tall arched cheekbones turning his face almost cadaverous. There were smudges of smoke on his chin and cheek, and the simple robe he was wearing showed evidence of charring around the sleeves. He looked up at the two of us on the stairs above him and his mouth opened in a silent 'O' of surprise.

The housekeeper was equally astonished. "My lady?" she queried, then her face narrowed down into lines of suspicion. "Is your business with the Master so urgent that you must disturb his wards to reach him?"

I waved my hand out in front of me in an easy movement. "There are no wards," I said. "I was sent by His Highness the Prince to ascertain the safety of his tutor, and I begin to wonder if there is more to this matter than might at first be thought."

"No wards?" She took a few hesitant steps towards me, then came the rest of the way in an anxious rush. The young man followed her with a frown of concentration, twisting his hands in an arcane gesture. Light glowed between them briefly, then Foo sneezed and the apprentice jumped, losing control of his spell so that the power was dispelled in a small shower of white sparks. The woman glared at him pointedly and he hurriedly stamped out the few glowing embers that had ignited the polished wood.

"Sorry, Theda," he muttered. "But she's right. There are no active wards, anywhere. I thought the house felt funny this morning."

"This is impossible," the housekeeper announced in some distress. "The Master always sets the wards. 'While I remain in this world, these wards remain.' He's always saying it – he's so possessive of his privacy, you see."

'While I remain ...' The quote chilled my blood, although Theda seemed unaware of its significance. Deckle, if that was the young man's name, realised the implications of the words almost as soon as they were spoken. He gave an incoherent cry and pushed past all of us to reach the top of the stairs. "MASTER?" he called as he ran, hurtling around the corner and down the corridor. "MASTER!" Foo and I took one look at each other and ran after him, leaving the housekeeper to stumble in our wake.

The apprentice did not go far. At the end of his chosen passageway was a pair of doors, the ornate carved kind that are usually the work of journeyman carpenters seeking their mastership. This pair were a match to the age of the house and carried arcane symbols among the curlicues at their edges. The doors themselves were cut into the shape of two sphinxes sat back-to-back. In the lintel above them was set a small globe, which lit the end of the corridor with pale amber light and cast shadows that added the illusion of life to the carvings. The youth stumbled to a halt under the mage light and heaved a sigh of relief. "He's not dead," he exclaimed, pointing upwards. "His soul flame still burns. And it burns strongly, too."

The upper floor was carpeted and my armoured heels drew no sound from the depths of its pile – an evidence of wealth that the ornate doors casually confirmed – but its luxury paled when compared to the source of its illumination. If the globe truly was a soul flame, and I had no reason to doubt that it was, then Reinwald well deserved the title of Archmagus. Such things took long and careful preparation, hours of patient work and application of skill and power. They reflected the inner health of their owner, dimming with sickness, or filling with swirling clouds that echoed turmoil and distress. The light above us was bright, but its colours shifted subtly as I watched, drifting from steady clarity to a faint flickering and back again.

"Does your master deal with spirits often?" I asked. Soulflames are not made for simple decoration, nor are they usually placed just to give light. For those who chose to converse with beings beyond the simple physical bounds they are an essential tool, anchoring a wielder's soul so that it cannot be lost or corrupted in realms men walk only with great peril.

Deckle shook his head. "Not now," he said. "He studied the summoner's art once, but not to any depth. There were too many other things he wanted to investigate for him to concentrate on just one. He says it's something you either master or you don't, and he didn't have the time to master it."

"No one ever does," Foo noted grimly. We have dealt more than once with those who mistakenly thought they could control what they called upon. That did not seem to be the case here, for which I was grateful.

One door was slightly ajar and I reached to push it fully open so that we could see what lay beyond. Deckle peered past my shoulder and gasped in horror and alarm.

Reinwald's workshop was a large high-vaulted chamber that ran the full depth of the house; windows on either side of the room let in the grey daylight. Stone walls jutted in from one corner, pierced by an arch and the hint of a spiral staircase beyond it – probably an entrance to the tower we had observed earlier. A pair of ornate double doors were set into the far wall, flanked by two single archways spaced evenly on either side. The air had a musty, strongly spiced smell to it, but that wasn't what had caused such consternation in the young man beside me. Stated simply, the place was a mess. Cabinets had been opened, their contents spilled out across nearby benches and the floor. Bookcases had been emptied, the volumes scattered about with total disregard for their value. Tapestries hung at odd angles where they had been ripped from their mountings to reveal symbol-painted walls beneath. Bottles and jars had been tipped over, their stoppers discarded and their contents spilled, while the shelves that had held them were festooned with lengths of parchment, pulled out of scroll cases and tossed away half opened. Scattered amongst the carnage were the larger pieces of the mage's equipment. Braziers and their stands leant against open chests from which fabric and other things spilled; a large globe sported an upturned bowl like an absurd hat; and a spoked wheel, big enough for an ale cart, hung from the outstretched paw of a huge stuffed bear that stood in one corner. Not even the mage's personal altar had been left unsullied: a carved image of the Celestial Magrix lay close to the now open doorway, one upraised arm broken off and missing.

"Oh, my," Theda exclaimed from behind us. "Whatever can have happened?"

Foo ducked easily under my still outstretched arm and dropped into a hunting crouch, his nose lifting to take in a long breath. "Mmm," he considered. "Decidedly fishy."

Leaving the apprentice and the housekeeper staring at the disaster I took a knee beside my companion. "Do you smell blood, or death?" I asked softly.

He shook his head. "This place has been empty for several hours," he said. His ears swivelled forward and his whiskers quivered in concentration. "There is no-one in the rooms beyond," he added, "and the door into the garden has been open for some time."

I glanced from one side of the room to the other. The balcony that we had observed on our walk around the house lay outside one wall of windows. A heavy curtain was half pulled across the length of the room on that side and part of it bulged out as if held slightly away from the wall. "What else can you tell me?"

His nose twitched and his mouth fell partly open as he once more drew the scents of the place across his sensitive palate. "There have been many oils spilt," he murmured, "and there are old smells of incense and fire ... One man is dominant, others hinted at." His thumb jerked back towards the apprentice as he spoke. "He may be one of them, but it's hard to say when he's stinking up the doorway with smoke. It's too much of a mixture to make much sense."

I nodded my thanks and started to rise. "You were right," I said. "This is decidedly fishy."

"That too." He grinned suddenly. "Oysters," he announced. "Fisher's Drop. Maybe Gutterside ... north of the river, in any case, and close to it I should think. Someone who lives there often enough to bring the taste of it with him."

I silently thanked my goddess for blessing me with such perceptive company, finally understanding his laughter on the stairs. I'd taken his words figuratively when he'd meant them literally. "Professional?" I hazarded. He shrugged.

"Past magical wards and under a mage's nose? I'd want to know what I was doing."

I had to agree. There was no doubt the room had been turned over very thoroughly. It still left the major question unanswered, however. What had happened to Reinwald? A thief might risk a lot for what some magical artifacts can fetch in places where questions don't get asked, but surely nobody would want to steal the Archmagus himself? I turned to Deckle, who was still staring at the chaos with definite signs of shock.

"This may be difficult for you to answer immediately," I began, "but can you tell me if anything might be missing?"

"Apart from the Master?" Theda demanded, recovering sufficiently to bustle past us and into the room. She shook her head in anxious despair and began to pick her way towards one of the archways on the other side. Foo rose to his feet and padded after her.

"I – I don't know," the young man managed after a moment. He looked around the room then opened his hands in a gesture of helplessness. "I suppose we ought to check the sanctuary. The Master keeps all of his most precious things in there."

I waved him into the room and he sidled past me, nervously avoiding the sprawl of books and papers that lay in his path. His hands flittered over the nearest table, picking things up and putting them down without direction. His expression was a devastated one. "How could anyone do such a thing?" he muttered. I had no easy answer for him. Theft is only an easy experience for those without a sense of value for anything. For this young man, who clearly understood the precious nature of much that his master possessed, the discovery that there might be people without such sympathies was heartbreaking.

I walked through the debris as carefully as I could, not wishing to add to the careless destruction. The intruder had apparently been looking for the most valuable things he could spirit away, leaving the larger and less portable treasures without a second thought. Reinwald's book collection alone was worth a small fortune, along with the precious herbs and oils that now stained its pages. Either the thief had had no idea of their value or else he was intent on things he could dispose of without the need for a specialist market.

"It's in here," Deckle said, pausing in front of the second set of carved doors. These were stone, not wood, and depicted coiled dragons lurking beneath a stylised image of our solar system. The carving of the central sun was dished outwards to form the handles of the doors, and the image of Dapre it supported was worn and indistinct. The apprentice hesitated before he reached to push at the stone, and I could understand that; Dapre was not my god, but it seemed a little sacrilegious to have to lay hands on his image merely to open a door.

He needn't have concerned himself. Both doors swung wide before his fingers even brushed the stone, a simple magical trigger easing their weight away from us and laying them quietly against the interior wall. It seemed Reinwald had not wanted to damage the carving further. Beyond lay a small octagonal room, the walls and ceiling painted in an unrelieved dark blue. There were no windows, and the only furniture was a single waist-high pillar at the very centre. This was topped by a black silk cushion, its centre dimpled as if it had recently held something of value, although it appeared to be empty now.

Deckle frowned at the empty silk, then moved past the pillar to lay his hands against one of the painted walls. "There are hidden doors," he explained, examining the spot he had chosen, "in each wall. There's a trick to ... Ah." Something had clicked within the structure and a small panel revolved out from the paint to reveal a triangular cupboard, lit by the pale glow of mage light. It contained a series of shelves on which were stood stoppered bottles, carved wooden boxes, and several other small items. "These haven't been touched," the apprentice realised with clear relief in his voice. He pushed that panel closed and moved on to examine the rest of the mage's hiding places. The first three seemed to be undisturbed; at the fourth he gave a small cry of anguish. "There are footprints in the dust," he said, pointing them out to me. I peered into the tiny space, seeing a clutter of boxes and a stack of books seemingly untouched on the shelves.

"Perhaps the Archmagus has moved something," I suggested. There were too many small and valuable items scattered on the middle shelf for the thief to have ignored if he had found this particular treasury. Deckle shook his head in puzzlement.

"It's the Master that puts the dust down to start with," he explained, "so we don't try to use things we aren't ready for yet. There are some boxes missing," he realised, reaching to count the accumulation of jewelled work that gleamed beside him. "I don't know what they were, though." He closed the panel carefully, making sure that no sign of it remained within the painted surface. I added the information to the growing pieces of my puzzle with a sense of quiet frustration. I wasn't looking for a thief, but for the mage he had burgled. There seemed to be no clues as to what might have become of him.

"He must have come in here," Deckle was deciding, still thinking on the theft. "He's taken the Star Diamond."

"What?" I looked round, to find him resting his hand on the silk pillow. "There was a diamond on that? Why didn't you say as much when we came in?"

The young man shrugged. "I was thinking about the magic things. I wasn't surprised that this was empty – it would be the most valuable looking piece in the place to an untrained eye. The Master always talked of it as a toy. It has an image," he demonstrated with his hands, "of the planets and everything. Right in the heart of it. But you have to look really closely to see it. Otherwise it's just a diamond."

I heard Foo snort with amused derision. "Young man," he growled as he appeared in the doorway, "to the sort that turned this place over there is no such thing as 'just' a diamond. He probably waltzed in here, saw a fortune in front of him and got out, as fast as his feet could carry him. It was money he was looking for, otherwise he'd have helped himself to some of the oils he spilt out there."

"Which still leaves the initial question unanswered," I said, moving across to join him in the opening. "Which is – where was the Archmagus while our Gutterside thief waltzed in and walked off with his prize?"

Foo shrugged, his nose twitching a little. "Not in his bedroom," he said. "The bed's not been slept in. Mind you, the candles were snuffed out, not left to burn away."

"The Master didn't use candles when he was working," Theda remarked. "He said that naked flame couldn't be trusted with power about. Where could he be? And whatever is he going to say when he sees all this?"

Deckle winced, which gave me a very good idea of Reinwald's potential reaction. "I will tell him," I promised. "When I find him. Is it likely anyone else in the house may know his whereabouts? Did anyone see him last night at all?"

Theda looked doubtful. "You can ask," she said slowly, "but I doubt it. The Master is very fond of keeping himself to himself."

"Gather everyone together," I requested. "I would like to know exactly what everyone was doing last night. They may have seen something without being aware of it. I would like a few moments to look around and then I will come down to join you."

"But," the housekeeper protested, "what about all this?"

"It's not going anywhere," Foo announced, catching her sleeve and leading her back towards the stairs. "You can clear up later." He threw me a wink as he went, a casual acknowledgement of camaraderie. Our flitter chase was turning out to be an interesting hunt after all, and he is never happier than when hunting.

Deckle trailed after the pair of them, leaving me to pace the disturbed workshop in an attempt to isolate some clue or other that would place me firmly on the trail. It was a thankless task. I knew very little of Reinwald's routine, or even of his life; the scattered chaos of his workshop revealed tantalising glimpses of a well-travelled man, equally well versed in his art. Among the debris I found letters from mages in Oscallon and Posmera, Daberon trade maps, bestiaries in a variety of languages, trinkets from as far north as Larrin and the Shattered Isles, and innumerable works of history with supporting commentaries. Apart from one or two of the letters, hardly any of it was recent; after a search that was fascinating but utterly unenlightening, I came to the conclusion that the Archmagus preferred to live in the past rather than the present. Wherever the man had gone he had not chosen to leave any clues behind him, and if there had been more subtle hints as to the events of the previous evening they had been lost in the thief's frantic searching.

I moved across to the windowed wall and the half-drawn curtain. Reinwald clearly showed no reluctance in demonstrating his wealth. Every window was glazed, and some of them were patterned with the fancy stained-glass that had become fashionable in the time of Alwick's father. The crystal blues and orange tints were a little too garish for my own tastes and had been replaced in more fashion-conscious houses by the subtle smoked greys and ambers beloved of our gentle queen. I doubted that Reinwald would be particularly conscious of fashion, unless it was that of some obscure historical period; I wondered if the presence of the windows in this large airy room had been one of his reasons for choosing the house in the first place.

The balcony door was ajar. I pulled the curtain back and found myself staring out at the sodden garden. Rain had soaked into the dark cloth down the line of the open door, and the polished wood below it was slick with damp. There were footprints faintly marked on the sill – traces of mud from the garden below, at a guess, although I couldn't tell who might have brought them there. The catch was a simple lift and turn affair, easy for a skilled burglar to work open from the outside – provided you could climb the outer stairs without being seen from the lower storeys, slip past a series of powerful magical wards without harm, and avoid alerting the reputedly testy mage inside the room. If he'd been inside the room, that was. For all I knew he'd been missing for several nights, not just one, and the thief had simply wandered in off the streets without realising what a fate-sent opportunity awaited him.

That line of thinking was getting me nowhere. I pushed the door shut gently and took a final walk around the room. The candles on the hanging candelabra were new and untouched, and yet there was wax spilt on the floor by the sanctuary doors. Someone had stood there with a lit candle recently, that much was clear. I doubted if the thief would have risked such a light for his ransacking. Whoever it was would have relied on moonlight; Athnea was high early in the evening, and Magrix had glowered low on the horizon all night. Either would have illuminated this windowed chamber with ease.

Nothing further came to enlighten me; it was as if the Archmagus had simply vanished into thin air. That wasn't exactly impossible, but the amount of power needed to achieve it would have left some evidence behind. I closed my eyes and extended my arms as I considered that, stretching my senses to their limit as I probed for the barest tingle of presence, the slightest touch of things unseen. All to no avail. Magic did linger in that place, but only so much as I would have expected in a house where it was practised and used almost every day. In fact, the lack of its presence in the workshop was more unsettling than finding it would have been. I let out my breath with a sigh and opened my eyes again. Foo's nose is far more reliable than my own sensitivity, and it hadn't so much as twitched since we had entered the room.

There was a mirror hanging on the wall opposite me; it reflected my image with impartial judgement as I walked towards it. Sometimes mirrors can be used as doorways, or other things (as Jarman had so unsettlingly discovered), but this one was simply imperfect glass and silver, its answer to my presence neither flattering nor cruel. I was an incongruity in the middle of the disruption, a precise figure of pale leather, shimmering chain and gleaming steel that had no place in a scholar's workshop. My reflection was all too familiar, yet I found myself pausing to consider it. Despite the greyness of the day, I gleamed like a piece of polished pewter from helm to heel: white and silver, the colours of my dedication, encased me as surely as the oaths I had taken so long ago. They wall me off from the everyday lives of others, both a barrier and a protection I can never escape, even if I so desired. In the mirror the stone at my throat was a glint of crystal, an inevitable reminder of the path I walked. No chain supports it; it sits against my skin like a glittering teardrop, a reminder of everything I have lost – and some of the things I have gained.

My silvered image stirred as I studied it, the bare ghost of a smile mocking my moment of introspection. I have no need of mirrors to remind me who I am. I have been my Lady's hand, her Avenger, for many years – and, besides, the picture was incomplete. I was armed, since there was a deadly blade balanced at my hip, but not with the weapon that had chosen me. The space at my back was empty, my soul sword safely locked within my tower. Dispiriter and I do not walk the streets of Nemithia together unless there is need for her; her kiss is always a final one.

I shook my self-analysis away with an impatient toss of my head and turned my attention back to the reflected chaos. Studying my own image was scarcely going to help find the Archmagus, however much it helped me find myself. I doubted I would have the need for any weapons on this particular hunt, and if I did then Dancer should serve my skills well enough. Information gathering was a task requiring diplomacy, subtle tact and ingenious questioning, not sword play or intimidation – although that has its place, should the demand arise.

The room had told me very little. I had to hope that the household could tell me more.

Chapter Three

"I was out last night. It was late when I returned and the house was in darkness. I made my own light to guide me to bed, and the griffin knows me so he gave no alarm."

Gregol Mac Doonin was the oldest of the apprentices, an Endorian both in name and in appearance. His night dark skin marked his ancestry clearly; he wore his hair plaited back in the Great Island style and the lilt of his accent placed his origins firmly on its soil. He looked older than the eighteen years he claimed, but then the pursuit of power carries many penalties. He had been the Archmagus' pupil for five years and his study would not have been easy.

"You saw nothing untoward? Nothing you might have considered strange?"

His laugh was deep, but its tone was wry. "My lady," he remonstrated, "I have studied many aspects of the Art – and it has been a long time since I thought of anything as 'strange'. I saw nothing I did not expect to see. Nor the lack of anything I did," he added, considering the matter carefully. I let him think. Student mages are schooled to pay attention to many things, and if there had been anything to see I would have expected it to have been seen by Mac Doonin. "No," he shook his head eventually. "Nothing. The griffin was chained at the main gate, the house was dark – and it was raining," he explained with the hint of a grin. "I dispelled my weather shield out in the street and ran for the porch, like I always do. The Master does not approve of the frivolous use of power."

My expression must have been faintly disapproving because he squirmed a little in his chair. I do not strictly approve of the trivial use of magic either, but at eighteen this young man had clearly not yet learned that power was something that you have to pay for. I doubted there was any harm in perfecting a usable shield against the

31

weather but wondered if it left him anything to defend himself with should the need arise. There have been many minor mages who have lost their lives simply because they chose to squander their skills on a little luxury. Then again, I considered, looking at the broad shoulders beneath the simply cut shirt, he might not think he needed the Art just to protect himself from footpads.

"What time was this?" I asked, deciding against any comment.

"Late. Second, or maybe third watch in the morning. I left the lower city just as the first was sounding, but we weren't in that much of a hurry."

"We?" I was interrupting him again, but his expression was hoping I hadn't noticed that particular slip of his tongue. He grimaced.

"I have – a friend," he said after a moment. "In the service of Val Vachea. We ... walked up the hill together. Took our time saying good night."

"In the rain," I reminded him. Midnight prayers and vigils aren't only good for the soul: they also keep me well informed about the local weather. There had been clear moonlight for most of the night, the clouds only arriving just before the dawn. The rain must have been a local phenomenon – and he'd likely been the one responsible for it. Weather magic can be difficult to master, and not that easy to control – but then again, young love is an impetuous thing. As an apprentice mage courting an earth witch he might well have been tempted to create an incentive that would bring the young lady closer to his side...

"In the rain," he agreed, looking a little sheepish. "But I saw nothing here. I swear it. The house was dark and I went straight to bed."

"Were the wards still active?"

"I don't know," he admitted. "I wasn't sober enough to notice."

I favoured him with the barest of smiles – a warm appreciation from me, although you have to know me well to know it. "At least you are honest, Apprentice

Mac Doonin. Thank you for your time. If you do recall anything else concerning last night, then let me know."

"I will," he said, rising to his feet. "I am worried about the Master. He has never left us without word before."

Deckle was next in the ranking, and the next I spoke to. His family name turned out to be Skatterbrow, after, he assured me, the hill outside his home village to the North. He could recall nothing either, having been immersed in his studies long into the night. I wasn't surprised he hadn't seen or heard anything; he struck me as the kind of scholar who would work unaware through an earthquake if the subject was enthralling enough. He had last seen Reinwald two days before, receiving instruction in the fire working he had yet to master. He would have regaled me with a blow-by-blow description of his efforts if I had not stopped him in mid flow.

He too was worried about his Master's absence, along with the riddle of the disturbed magic pieces in their hidden compartments. He told me again that he had no way of knowing what might be missing, but that most items would be useless to anyone unless they knew the words or methods that would spark their power. Reinwald, he assured me, did not leave active magic unattended; he had ways of ensuring that even permanently enchanted pieces would slumber until he chose otherwise. This was fascinating information, but not particularly helpful. All but the ineptest of pot wizards have ways of determining commands and triggers for such things, even if they have no hope of matching one quarter of the power of those who made them. There are those in Oscallon who devote themselves to such studies, exploring the workings of ancient mages and taking years to decipher the barest aspect of uncommon artifacts.

After Deckle came Hal Markstele – a mere lad, younger than Jarman and no less nervous. He had been with the Archmagus only a year and was still struggling with learning to read. He had been in bed early and had heard no-one other than Theda and Eachan moving about in the house after dark. As the youngest apprentice, his duties were exhaustive and he had obviously been well asleep by the time the unknown thief had come to call. I was learning very little, and nothing that hinted at what might have become of Reinwald.

The other members of the household proved to be no more enlightening. The maid, a timid and plain young woman with no claim to distinction in any manner, answered my questions with monosyllabic terror. She slept in the back room behind the scullery. She had heard nothing all night. She had not seen Reinwald for several days. She took her orders from the housekeeper, or from Eachan. He had sent her to her room early because she had helped herself to the cold cuts set out for the apprentices. She had stayed there until first light, when she was charged with checking the fires. She hadn't gone upstairs; she never went upstairs and she went quite white at the thought of it. Her master clearly terrified her.

After I dismissed the maid I spoke to the cook, who lived out in the lower city and had left soon after curfew watch, and then to the housekeeper. Theda bustled in and dipped an automatic curtsey in my direction before moving across to take the chair I was indicating. The courtesy was one of habit rather than intent, the inevitable dipped response from a servant in authority to one they might be expected to serve. I considered her thoughtfully as she took her seat, deciding that her seeming diffidence towards my rank was probably due more to her distracted state than anything else.

"My lady," she said politely, folding her hands in her lap. Her expression was set into firm composure, a deliberate assumption of calm beneath which seethed a noticeable anxiety. I could not decide whether she was concerned for her master, disturbed by the disruption of her household, or expected to be blamed for whatever had occurred; the only thing I was sure of was that, for once, I was not the cause of my company's discomfiture.

"You are…?" I prompted.

"Theda Dagspan. I have kept the Archmagus's house

for fifteen years – ever since he took up residence on the Hill."

"I see. So you know Reinwald and his habits well, I take it."

She bristled slightly, a reaction she pushed away leaving only a hint of annoyance in her eyes. "The Master is very insistent on routine," she said primly. "And I do my best to comply with his wishes, if that is what you mean."

I didn't react to her indignation, although I suspect Foo might have done. I had intended no impropriety by the suggestion. "Were the last three days any exception – to your routine, that is?"

She thought about it. "No. I attended to the daily chores, as usual. The maid and I went to the market the day before yesterday, and I paid the calling tradesmen the day before that. The Master quite often retires to his private rooms for days on end. He keeps a cold store in his study so he has access to food and drink when he is working. I made sure it was well stocked only a few days ago, so I did not expect to see him unless he had need of me. The house and the wellbeing of the apprentices are my concerns, not my master's business."

I nodded, thoughtfully. There was no doubting the fierce pride with which she regarded those concerns. "Have there been any visitors this week?"

"Apart from yourself, my lady? Only two. It was after the Lord Lythian attended him that the Master retired to his rooms – and," she dimpled suddenly, "the Prince of the House of Scarlet called later that same day. I told him the Master had asked not to be disturbed, so he didn't stay," she added, a hint of disappointment in the admission. I frowned. Neither of those august gentlemen were likely to be responsible for the devastation that lay in the rooms above us.

"And nobody called last night? An old friend, a stranger leaving no name, a client?"

"Nobody," she insisted firmly. "I cannot understand this, my lady. The Master never leaves without giving word of his absence, never. And that mess upstairs ... I shall never get it back to how it was." I was not sure which she saw as the greater problem – Reinwald's unexplained absence, or the task of reordering the chaos of his room before he returned. "He will be furious."

"You have no cause to fear his wrath, unless you had a hand in raising it," I observed mildly. She bristled for a second time, favouring me with an expression that would have been an offended frown if she wasn't trying to stay polite.

"The Master," she said archly, "has entrusted me with his household. He desires order at all times, everything at its proper time and in its proper place. This... this... *violation* of his harmony will anger him beyond all measure. So many things spoiled, so much work disrupted ..."

"The Archmagus will learn the truth of these events." I interrupted what sounded like the beginnings of a tirade with firm words. "Once I have unravelled this tangle and found the answers in it for myself, I will explain matters to him. As soon as I locate him, I promise you."

She looked slightly taken aback by the certainty of my tone. "As my lady wishes," she decided, although her eyes suggested that I might be taking on a task which could prove beyond me. I did not bother to enlighten her. Finding Reinwald was going to be much harder than dealing with his ire once I had done so, and I have little reason to fear any but the most powerful of sorcerers. It was clear that she could tell me nothing further, and so I dispatched her to begin her self-appointed task in the rooms above.

That left only one more for me to interview. Foo followed him in, the two of them bringing the sharp scent of late autumn air to cut through the cloying warmth of the heavy coal fire. The man who had greeted us at the gate had been showing my companion the garden, and Foo had a rime of moisture clinging to the surface of his fur. He loped across to the hearth and shook himself vigorously, leaving his escort to make his way to where I sat. Eachan was a compact figure, well-muscled beneath the wool and leather jerkin he wore. He looked to be in his middle years, and the lines of his face spoke of a man used to outdoor work; the easy fluid movement with which he sank into the indicated chair implied I might be in the presence of a warrior. He looked at me challengingly, his eyes dark and uneasy in his weather-worn face. He held his right arm awkwardly, I realised, and managed not to stare, considering his face instead. After a moment he relaxed a little and shrugged, somewhat lopsidedly.

"I thought you might say something," he announced. "He did." His head jerked in Foo's direction and I saw the curve of his ears flatten down and back, although he remained intent on the fire.

"Should I?" I asked. Eachan glowered moodily at the floor as he answered.

"Those that realise do," he said. "I shouldn't mind, but mostly they can't imagine what it's like. I was a swordsman," he went on, the statement proud and a little bitter. "I was good, too. 'Til the cold drake withered my arm half away. He killed the thing –" an emphasis on the 'he', somehow managing to convey an image of Reinwald without a mention of his name, "– but it was too late. The Seeker priests healed me as best they could, but they couldn't make it the way it was."

He was waiting for my sympathy, wanting to throw it back in my face. I knew, from his expression, that there would be nothing I could say to ease the anger that he nurtured within him. It was unfortunate that I was sworn to the goddess who had tried to help and, in his eyes, failed him; but all the goodwill in the world cannot turn the traveller from the path of fate, only smooth his way as the gods allow. It had been written that this man lose the skill he had prized, and while the intervention of prayer had healed his body, only inner peace can heal the soul.

"You are not a Seeker, I take it," I said, reading my answer in the embittered flash of his eyes. "Do you follow any gods?"

He laughed hollowly. "Only Reinwald. He took me in – gave me work, trusted me with his confidence. Religion does not put food in your belly, or clothes on your back. Only strength can do that."

This was neither the time nor the place to answer that argument; in any case I doubted Eachan would hear my words. I have never had any doubt that the gods provide, but not in the way that many an awe-struck peasant would believe. Miracles only happen to those who truly offer something in return, and the price is never cheap, no matter what the priests may say.

"How long have you served the Archmagus?" I asked, directing my questions to the matter in hand. He considered his answer carefully.

"Five years with my sword, three without. It's nothing fancy, you understand – a little fetch and carry, caring for the horses, keeping an eye on things – nothing a cripple with a strong back can't manage well enough."

He was trying to bait me, emphasising his condition with deliberate and cynical bitterness. I heard Foo hiss quietly to himself, torn between his sympathy for the man's fate and anger at his behaviour. I chose to ignore both the reaction and the words that had elicited it.

"When did you see him last?"

"Reinwald? I can't say for sure. Sometime yesterday, I suppose. I remember seeing him up in the tower round about noon – checking the sun or something. But he wasn't there last night. Too overcast for stargazing – and too cold. Likes to work in comfort, he does. And you need a good reason to disturb him, too." His words held a hint of wry remembrance, as if he recalled the occasion when he had learned that particular lesson.

"You had no such reason last night?"

"Reason?" He smiled without humour. "What reason would I have to disturb the mighty Archmagus at his study? I'm only the stable boy – not one of his learned company. They know so much, ask them where he's gone."

It appeared that Eachan was as bitter about Reinwald's

charity as he was about the reason for it. I wondered why he had stayed in the mage's service for as long as he had. "I am asking you at the moment," I reminded him gently. He glowered back, the look half sulk, half contempt. "Last night," I suggested, realising I would get nowhere by responding to his barely concealed resentment, "you heard nothing to remark on? Nothing that might have been a thief pursuing his handiwork?"

He sat forward, his expression suggesting I should mind my own business. "I sleep above the stable, not in the house. The only thing I heard last night," he explained testily, "was Prentice Gregol, running across the courtyard some time in the third watch. He'd been out," he added, his tone daring me to contradict him.

"I know." I sighed, finding nothing enlightening in any of the testimony I had managed to gather together. Eachan seemed to confirm Mac Doonin's account of himself, and it would seem that nobody had had any sight of Reinwald since noon the day before. "Thank you, Eachan. If you recall anything else that might be of help to use, I would be glad to hear it."

"I'm sure you would." He rose to his feet with an easy gesture and stared at me for a moment; then he laughed softly and walked away with a warrior's swagger in every step. Foo waited for the door to close before he drew in an angry hiss of breath.

"By the Wolf below," he growled, striding over to join me, "if he had two good arms I'd call him to account for that!" His ears were almost flat with fury and his whiskers were bristling.

I shook my head gently, finding him a brief smile. "If he had two good arms, my friend, he would have no cause to carry such bitterness. He isn't worth the trouble – at least," I corrected myself, "he doesn't think so. That is why he's so angry at the world."

Foo let his ears relax, but his tail twitched as he leapt to perch on the table, and his claws curled out as his fingers grasped at its edge. "The garden," he announced, "is wet. And tells me nothing much. Our thief may have come in

39

through the side gate, but it has rained since and taken most of the traces away. Odd though," he remarked, reaching to groom the fur beneath his chin with a curl of clawed fingers, "our intruder took mud into the workshop with him, and last night was dry until the early hours."

My lips quirked in what he would know was a wry smile. "Here, it rained. Mac Doonin was courting last night and conjured a reason to get closer to his company."

Foo's whiskers twitched and his mouth opened in a slow panted grin. "Ahh," he purred. "A young man with cunning, then?"

I nodded, resting my elbow on the tabletop to let my chin slump into my hand. "But no-one claims to have seen Reinwald since midday yesterday. If I wanted to pursue a puzzle with no clues, I'd be hard put to find one more challenging."

"Someone," Foo suggested gently, "has been lying to you."

I allowed myself a short snort of laughter. "Most of them, probably. Little lies cloud the truth with more efficiency than large ones, my friend. Mac Doonin was undoubtedly out without his master's permission, and Eachan – Eachan cannot see his own truths, so I should not expect any honesty from him at all. There may be many answers hidden in this house, but we do not possess the key to any of them."

Foo reached to brush the lingering dampness away from his ears, combing at his fur with casually extended claws. "When you can't open a locked door with a key," he grinned. "What do you do instead?"

I let the question settle in the air between us, turning to share the thought that spurred it with the golden glint in his eyes. "Break it down?" I suggested as innocently as I could muster. He wasn't fooled for a moment; his ears flicked back in mock disgust at my failure to grasp his reasoning.

"Barbarian," he growled. "In civilised society, we look for a thief – and get him to pick the lock."

Chapter Four

"One particular thief – in the whole of Gutterside? My lady, you must be joking. Without a name or a face to put to the job, it could have been practically anybody. This isn't the Parade Quarter, you know. Honesty is a secondary virtue on this side of the city."

"I heard it was a positive handicap," Foo remarked, favouring the speaker with wide and guileless eyes. The man barked a half laugh in return.

"You may be right," he said, unoffended at the implication. He is a broad-shouldered figure, blessed with a level of energy that belies his years. Kirby served as a Captain of Infantry in the Skirmish Wars and chose to buy out of military service once that flare of conflict had been reduced to diplomatic growling across borders. He'd spent less than two years in retirement before presenting himself to the office of the City Prefects in search of a way to restore some order to his chosen neighbourhood. They'd listened to his complaint for less than a minute; he'd found himself with a commission in the Nemithia Militia, and the task of whipping a beleaguered and undermanned unit back into the semblance of an ordered Wardhouse. That he had succeeded had been no surprise to the men under his command; his decision to turn down the resultant offer of promotion had startled the Prefects considerably.

I have known Kirby for many years. We fought together once, in the shadow of the Harren Hills; he had admired the fact that I did not weep over the men that I lost, and I had admired the honesty which allowed him tears. We met again during the business of the Silver Sailor, soon after he had taken charge of his district. Alwick might rule Asconar and bestride his City of Nemithia with noble authority, but in Gutterside it is Kirby who keeps the reins tight.

41

"I can ask around," he continued thoughtfully. "There's been a few rumours lately about mage-work surfacing in places it doesn't belong, but I've been a little too busy to bother tracking them down. That may have been a mistake."

"You don't make mistakes," I pointed out. "Just judgements. I did not have much hope of enlightenment in our search. This matter we have found ourselves tangled in may have to remain a mystery."

Kirby leant back in his chair and studied me with the admiring eye he reserves for those who have earned his respect. "I have found that it isn't usually a good idea to meddle in the affairs of Archmages," he said. "Too many unpredictable things can start happening to you. Even the average enchanter is dangerous, in my opinion. Playing with fire, that's what I say. Sorcery is all very well, but you can't rely on it. Not like a solid blade," he added, patting at the hilt against his hip. Foo's mouth opened in a wide grin of silent laughter – anybody who knew the man also knew the tale of that sword, and where he got it from. It was Karhad work, and it had been stolen so many times its original owner was long forgotten. He'd carried it for several months before circumstance had revealed the manner of its enchantments; he'd simply named it 'Stonecutter' and put it back into its sheath.

"We are scarcely meddling in Reinwald's affairs," I sighed. "We can't even find him." I started to rise, reluctantly. I enjoy Kirby's company when I have the time to find it. His soldier's approach to things is a welcome relief from the intricate dance of courtly protocol. At that moment the door to the office was flung open and a grim-faced man in the Wardhouse uniform strode in. He was halfway across the room before he realised his commanding officer had company; hesitation flittered across his features and his step faltered visibly. "Ah, Captain…"

"Spit it out, Barboff," Kirby barked impatiently. He had given orders we were not to be disturbed.

"Sir. There's a runner come in from Packers Street,

with word of a domestic up in the attics. Raised voices and screaming. The third patrol went to sort it out."

"I should hope so," Kirby growled. "Why bother me with it? I have guests."

"Yes, sir. But it's the same place we've been watching for a week, over that business of the package in from Carthery, and Iglen thought..."

"Iglen thinks too much," our friend muttered with annoyance. "All right, all right, we'll go take a look. I'm sorry, my lady. Duty calls."

I nodded my thanks and finished gaining my feet. "It was a simple query, my friend. Don't let it take you from your routines. I know only too well that you do not work your particular magic from behind a desk."

"Magic!" Kirby laughed as he led us to the door. "Sweat and hard work, more like. I'll be right there, Barboff. Fetch Iglen and his bag of tricks and we'll go see what mess we have to clean up this time."

The man saluted and sprinted away down the passage of the wardhouse in search of Kirby's resident wizard. Despite his remarks concerning sorcery, the captain had been one of the first to embrace Alwick's suggestions regarding the availability of magical advice to the City Wardens. Iglen is a pot wizard, one of those with a smattering of talent and an overwhelming curiosity. He'll never match the reach of Reinwald's power, but he provides a certain protection to the common man at arms, and his simple spells are good enough to aid in the minor matters that the Watch deals with on a day-to-day basis.

Foo was looking at me with expectancy, as if he had read more into the news than the captain had. I threw my faithful companion a puzzled frown, wondering what he was thinking, then my mind replayed Barboff's words and revelation dawned. "Captain," I said, as Kirby bowed in intended farewell, "did your man just mention Carthery?"

"He did," the warrior affirmed, his face a little puzzled. "There's a lot of traffic comes up the river; you know that. If anything is brewing in Gutterside it inevitably has the taint of Black Velvet in it. Half our folk have relatives of some sort on the delta – don't read more into it than that, my lady."

"Alwick is meeting the Duke at the Hawksley Lodge," Foo murmured softly, his ears swivelling to check that only Kirby and I were close enough to hear him. "On the third day of the month of the Birch."

I watched the man do the inevitable mental calculation as he translated the lunar month into the solar one; Foo has never got out of the habit of using the Tree Cycle when naming time, even when given the date on the Ascorian calendar. "That's less than a month away," Kirby realised. "I hadn't heard that the King would be leaving Nemithia during Dosefar."

"He won't be," I said dryly, ushering him out of his office and in Barboff's wake. "You haven't heard anything concerning Duke Octian, either. Suffice it to say that we have an interest in anything that might bear the taint of Black Velvet, as you so eloquently put it. This business of Reinwald will not hurt to be put aside for the moment. You may have more pressing matters for me to attend to."

The captain thought that one over as he led us out into the courtyard. Like me, he detests the necessities of politics, but he appreciates that like and need do not always sit together comfortably. To my mind the city of Carthery squats like an unwelcome canker on Asconar's western border, and would be better simply ploughed back into the swamp that gave it birth. Alwick, who is a shrewd King and a better politician than many give him credit for, is more inclined to bargain with an untrustworthy Duke than he is to make war on the Velvet City the man commands. He's probably right; more good men would lose their lives in such a battle than would gain from Carthery's downfall, but that doesn't mean I have to like it. I knew that there need only be the barest whiff of treachery and all of the careful negotiations would slide back into the muck of the delta; I wasn't sure if I was hoping to find such evidence, or desperately hoping I wouldn't.

Foo was grinning at me and I resisted the temptation to turn and glare at him. Kirby might be a friend, and loyal to the king, but the R'rruthren really had no right to announce Alwick's business as if he were discussing the posted times for Market Day. I wasn't even sure how he knew about the meeting, although I wasn't surprised that he did. Many folk take Foo for granted at court, or even treat him as if he were a dumb animal. The foolish ones, that is.

Barboff and Iglen were waiting outside the watch house with three other men, the unmistakable figure of the mage muttering to himself in the way he often did. The deep blue of his overrobe, edged with a hint of sky-coloured braid, flapped around his bony frame; its hood was pulled up against the autumn air. Militia wizards wear Warden livery of course, the colours a match to the tabards and trappings his companions sported over their practical leathers and mail. Barboff had the man's bag under his arm, since Iglen has never been strong enough to carry his own paraphernalia, and its owner was eyeing him with looks that threatened all kinds of dire fate should anything happen to it. Kirby glanced from one to the other, sighed with forbearance and beckoned them both over. "This had better not take long," he decided, glaring at the scraggly wizard as he did so. "I have a number of things to do today."

"Trust me," Iglen giggled. He couldn't help that. It was a nervous reaction to authority, not deliberate disrespect. He glanced at me warily as I stood behind his captain's shoulder and giggled again, a high pitched sound that made Barboff wince. I returned the glance with calm assessment; I actually like Iglen, although he may not know it. There is a shrewd mind behind the bespectacled and nervous façade, and although he might not be a powerful mage, his knowledge of forensic magic is unmatched this side of Oscallon.

"Don't I always?" Kirby sighed, and led the way out into the rain.

***

45

Packers Street turned out to be one of those twisted lanes that wind their way through Gutterside with complete disregard for planning or space. Houses jostled beside warehouses, shops and stables, their superstructures rising over our heads to form a tunnelled roof, which at least gave some shelter from the autumn drizzle. I have heard it said that the tiered houses in Nemithia arise from some obscure law which taxes the ground floor area, rather than the overall size of a building. Whatever the reason, there are parts of the city that are crowded with houses whose upper storeys jut out over the lower ones; in the merchant quarter bargains are said to be made between guilds without either party leaving their own building, it being possible to reach out and shake hands across the street from the upper windows. It is said that, in places, it might be possible for inventive lovers to do a lot more than simply shake hands between one window and the next; Packers Street took this theory to an extreme.

The buildings were a jumble of style and intent, no two the same from one side of the street to the other. Three and four storeyed labyrinths dominated their lower neighbours and many of the older, square-built warehouses had become the foundations for ramshackle upper apartments that lurked in among the angled, sloping roofs. In places it was hard to see where one building ceased and the next one began. It wasn't just the buildings that crowded the street: there were far more folk about their business here than there had been in the High City. Figures scurried from the tramp of efficient feet as Kirby and his men swept down the centre of the narrow thoroughfare. Others stepped into secluded doorways or glared down from half shuttered windows. There are many people in the lower districts who have reason to dislike the Wardens, but most of them are sensible enough to retain a modicum of respect for their presence. Kirby they knew only too well, and there were those who greeted him as our procession passed. Foo picked a fastidious path beside me, managing to keep a wary eye on all the spectators at the same time as avoiding stepping into anything too questionable on the cobbles under his feet. I have no doubt that he and I were the reason for many of the stares that were received that day; I have walked in Gutterside on other occasions, and undoubtedly Foo knows the place better than I, but Packers Street was not the sort of avenue either of us would normally choose to walk quite so openly in the middle of the day.

Street urchins gathered into huddles as the Wardens strode past, then scurried after us with wary curiosity. Beggars looked up in hope before turning their heads away at the sight of the uniforms. My hand dipped to the pouch at my belt at the first of these, then I let it drop down to my sword hilt instead. Those who chose to beg in such places were likely to be less than worthy of any charity; the honest and the truly needy know that the chapels and the houses of healing are always open to them. There were signs of genuine industry in among the ragged occupants: half mended nets hung from some windows and stall holders offered titbits and other items from trays or barrows in the places where the street widened into an attempt at a square. Other hawkers lurked on the corners of side streets and passageways, their sales more discrete, and their wares less openly displayed. None of them were Kirby's business that day – or mine, either – but I expect both he and his men took careful note of who stood where, and with whom. Men hurried past, or stood aside for us, burdened with a variety of goods, and cautious looking characters with well-worn sword hilts walked among them with suspicious eyes. Women were less in evidence, most of those we saw being cloaked against the inclement weather or gossiping in doorways and across the upper floors above us. Once a splash of something tumbled from above with a cry of "'ware below!" and the patrol stepped aside from its descent without a pause in their hurried pace. Iglen looked up, and Barboff dragged him on, while Foo hissed at the suspect puddle and wrinkled his nose with distaste. I skirted it with easy steps, my cloak shaking off a stray splatter or two, and caught the way that a rigid twitch of my companion's tail encouraged his own cloak to do the same. Foo is one of the cleanest creatures I know, far cleaner than many of the court dandies who strut their perfumed figures with such pride; he hates getting dirty unnecessarily, and he hates getting wet even more. A little rain he doesn't mind, if circumstances dictate it, but he generally prefers to be both clean and dry. That he achieves both in even the direst of situations has never ceased to amaze me, and I recall the few occasions in which fate has directed otherwise with a solidly *private* amusement; much as he might suffer such indignity, the idea of being laughed at because of it would wound his pride to the core.

We found the house we sought about halfway along the twisted street, set back a little way from the main line of buildings in a semi-mews. It was a three or four-storey structure built from rough-hewn timber and hemmed in by others of its kind, the jutting levels concealing the roofs above. A burly figure in Ward uniform stood firmly in the main doorway, and he drew to a smart salute as Kirby strode across to join him.

"All quiet, Gosden?" the captain asked, and the man nodded.

"The Lieutenant's on the upper floor, sir," he reported. "You have to take the outer stairs because the inner doesn't go that high. There's a body, sir," he added helpfully as his superior turned to eye the makeshift timber work that formed the outer access route. Kirby glanced back with dry unsurprise.

"Really," he growled. "Thank you, Gosden. Stand to your post."

"Sir!" Gosden saluted a second time, earning himself a series of jeers and catcalls from the small crowd that inevitably gathers when the Wardens do. His fellow officers threw him unsympathetic looks and started on the business of dispersing the onlookers. Kirby straightened his shoulders and started up the steps, which creaked rather ominously under his weight. Iglen went a little white. Foo glanced upwards and then across the street before bounding after Kirby's ascent; the stairway bore his lithe weight somewhat better than the man ahead of him and he went up at a fair pace, able to pounce onto the rail and up onto the first turn just as the captain reached it. Kirby paused and growled something as the R'rruthren hurtled past him, then leant out over the drop and beckoned me, Iglen and Barboff to come up. The wizard vented a martyred sigh, picked up the hem of his robe and started up the steps, using his twisted staff to test the firmness of the treads before he stood on them. Barboff hefted the leather bag onto his shoulder and followed. He kept more than a duty eye on the frail figure's progress, I noted, and decided that the officer's respect for the man was a little deeper than surface impression might suggest. I waited until they too had turned the first landing before I set my steps to follow them. Not that it was strictly necessary – since I do not have Kirby's bulk, and my armour is much lighter than looks imply – but Iglen was nervous enough about the stairs without my ascent unnerving him further.

The delay gave me a chance to consider the eyes that watched our investigation; idlers' eyes mostly, a gathering that would be questionable had it been made without apparent reason. One out of four met my gaze without turning aside, and only one in three of those were self-assured enough to answer my consideration with confidence. Some of that was arrogance, less was simple honesty; the youngest among them stared back with open fascination until his mother swept him up and away. An elderly man smiled at me and nodded his respect, while others merely watched me warily. The badge of King's Investigator is not one I wear openly, but I am sufficient of an oddity to be known in many circles that would not recognise any of my fellows; Nemithia is full of lurid tales of my exploits, most of which are highly exaggerated, and no doubt many gathered there were busy trying to decide if I were as dangerous as they had heard.

I am, but I had no intention of proving it – or reason, either. I swept them all the barest of bows and strode up the stairs, the bells on my cloak jingling and my heels ringing as they hit the suspect wood. A murmured sigh ran around the crowd before they began to melt back into the houses. The Wardens hustled them on; even as I reached the second turn the more usual street cries began to re-echo through the briefly startled streets.

The top landing was part of a wide balcony that ran along the front of several buildings, allowing access to the gabled roofs and the attics they enclosed. The ceiling of Gutterside was a city in itself, stepped slates and thatched angles jostling for dominance as they practically collided above the twisting street below. Here, above the mews, there was sufficient space for a street all its own, a wooden walkway that served a whole community of doors and shutters exposed to the grey light of a day that would fail to dispell the shadows by the time it reached the ground below. The wood was wet, slick with the day's drizzle, and there was a wind, of sorts, that cut through cloth and added to the sense of misery that lingered here. Barboff stood at a narrow doorway, its frame filled with the splintered remains of what might have once been a door. With him was another figure I knew – Lieutenant Treacher, leader of the Gutterside Third Patrol and Kirby's trusted second in command. He saluted as he recognised me and greeted me with a weary smile.

"A long climb for little gain, my lady," he said. "I should have known you'd be with the captain when I saw that furry friend of yours arrive. They are within, but I would caution you that what waits is not a pretty sight."

I acknowledged his greeting with a polite nod. "I am not a vaporous maiden, expecting beauty in the middle of a midden, friend Treacher. I have seen carnage that would strike you to the soul – I doubt one corpse will offend my sensibilities."

He grinned and stood aside to let me pass. Barboff was looking a little green around the face, and I wondered how old he was. First impression had placed him in his twenties, but perhaps he not been in the Militia itself overlong. He moved as if to protest at my entry, but Treacher held him back with a casual hand. "Step carefully within," the lieutenant advised, "Iglen does not like to be disturbed when he is working."

The room was sparsely furnished, a bare-boarded attic that might have been roomy but for the sloping ceiling and the intrusive chimney breast. It boasted three windows, all of them open, and all looking out onto the jumble of rooftops. Daylight filtered in, along with a vague view of the distant palace and Raven's Hill rising beyond it. Foo was perched on the sill of one of the windows, one eye fixed on the scene at the centre of the floor, one ear cocked to catch some sound or other from outside. His hand rested on the hilt of a throwing knife and his whole stance was wary and alert. Kirby stood to one side of him, leaving space for the shuffling mage as he circled the area, and in the middle of the room itself...

I have seen death in many forms. This one wasn't that unusual. The man lay on his back, his head tipped to one side and his hands sprawled loosely on his stomach, as if they had slipped from the hilt of the knife which sprouted from between his ribs like a weed struggling between paving stones. Blood pooled under him and soaked the leather of his clothing, adding to the unmistakable stench of death that hung in the air. A quick, if nasty death, the knife sinking deep and piercing the heart. The victim was dressed in unremarkable clothing: leather breeches, a loose shirt, and a padded leather jerkin, currently unlaced. He was of an age that might fit comfortably between the late twenties and the early forties: a man born and bred in the lower city, or a place like it, his weathered and beaten features half hidden behind a rough cut beard.

"Seen one, you've seen a hundred," Kirby remarked resignedly. "Men like him and the deaths to match. Don't often find them this warm, though, and rarely in their own homes. We're usually digging them out of the gutter."

"Quiet," Iglen muttered with annoyance. He was using the man's blood to etch a series of symbols on the bare floor around the body, painting the patterns with the pointed end of his staff. Occasionally he would toss some powder or other over a completed figure, and he was frowning as he worked, his lips moving in a complicated repetition of sound.

"Iglen thinks the corpse is fresh enough to generate an image," Kirby whispered, sliding across to join me. "He doesn't get the chance to work this kind of casting very often – usually we're working with vague sympathies. A blood match, or a rough approximation. A full reconstruction needs a lot of energy to power it."

"And I'll be useless for days," the wizard snapped, straightening up and glaring at him. "Can I work here? Sir?"

"Carry on," Kirby allowed with a wave of his hand and a pained expression. He values Iglen highly, but there are times when the man's manner lacks both patience and respect. I can't say I blame him; he must fight for what power he has, and it does not come easily. His irritability at such times is probably due to his need to prepare himself for an effort that an Archmagus like Reinwald would achieve with the barest flick of one finger.

Foo's fur was bristling slightly, and I doubted it was entirely due to the impending use of power. His nose was atwitch as well and the tip of his tail was trembling with an alertness that hinted at an unease he could not place. I took the opportunity to take a closer look at my surroundings, wondering what had alerted him, and why. I have said the room was sparsely furnished; it contained a low bed, still unmade, a small table, two wooden chests and three chairs. The bed was covered by a hastily flung blanket, its edges trimmed with fur, and the sheets beneath had a look of quality that belied the shabby appearance of both the room and the man. The table had been covered with papers and other items, most of which seemed to have been violently swept to the floor, leaving a toppled tankard and a single withered rose in a pool of clear liquid. The chests had also been flung open; silk as well as leather and wool trailed out of them. Their contents spoke of a feminine presence, as well as the silent man in their midst – scarlet brocade mingled with working gear, and slim strapped sandals lay in among the wreckage. The items that Iglen ignored as he continued to make his way around the sprawl of death were mostly unimportant: pewter plates and tumbled hunks of bread lay spattered with blood beside the man who had had no time to finish his last meal. There were incongruities, however. An expensive silvered fork, Kharad work, had been discarded among the other cutlery, and there was a salt cellar, spilling white salt onto equally white chicken meat, both luxuries for this end of the city, and both an unlikely find in a rented room such as this. The dead man had had money, and recently by the looks of it: unless, of course, all three items had been stolen.

Iglen reached the end of his circling and paused to lift his scrawny arms in a dramatic gesture. Foo sneezed, earning himself a despairing look, and Kirby and I pressed ourselves back against the wall as the wizard summoned his concentration. The room darkened; mist rolled up from the archaic runes scattered across the floor, and a vague image of the dead man slowly materialised above his silent figure. Kirby's eyes grew grim. Alive, the man had more certainty about him, the careful look of a man who did not like to work for his living. The image shifted as the man waved a hand towards the window, turning towards the door with movement on his lips. There was no sound, and the image wavered in and out as sweat beaded Iglen's furrowed brows. I held my breath, conscious of the work that was wrought here, waiting to glimpse the accusation that the spell would raise.

It was not long in coming. A second figure drifted into the circle of rust coloured smoke: a taller man, draped in black leather and wool and assured in his movements. The dark cowl tipped back, revealing an angular face with a dark smudge of beard and a scarred cheek above it; the man's hand shot out, seizing the first figure with contempt. They argued, the first denying, the second accusing. Blows were exchanged, so that the image wavered and reformed as the quarrel moved into and out of the circle. Iglen was shaking visibly as he fought for control. Finally the two figures stood together in the very centre of the room; reluctantly our dead man lifted something from his pocket and held it out to his visitor. A brief and ugly smile twisted the dark man's lips. With one hand he took what was offered; with the other he twisted a knife from his belt and drove it home as casually as if he stabbed at meat on a spit.

A woman screamed. Iglen reeled back, and the image shattered with a flare of blood red light. I blinked once, to clear my eyes, just in time to see Foo hurl himself from the window and onto the rain slicked roof outside. Kirby cursed, and Lieutenant Treacher dived in from outside, his sword drawn. Barboff was a scant step behind him. They were in time to catch the wizard as he collapsed, his face pale and his breath coming in ragged gasps.

I cast one short glance at the tumbled wizard before I ran across to the window that Foo had vacated so hurriedly. His claw marks were fresh on the wooden sill, and his cloak lay where he had flung it aside – but there was no sign of him, or the owner of the voice that had so dramatically interrupted us.

"Midras be merciful," Kirby announced with clear astonishment. I turned in alarm; the corpse that had lain so certainly upon its back was now turned onto its side, and beneath it, clean of the blood that was now slowly pooling towards it, lay a slim leather bound book. The captain's astonishment had to be for the movement of a dead man; mine for was what it revealed. I had seen other such volumes, not so long since. They were, as was this, bound in dark leather and glided at their edges and they all, including this one, bore on their polished surface the imprint of a coiled griffin.

The mark of Archmagus Reinwald.

Chapter Five

"The hunt went hunting all around; across the roofs and round the town." Foo was laughing silently, his dagger tipped jaws opened as he panted for breath. The line was an old one, a song for children drawn from an older legend, and it brought a smile to Kirby's face.

"She doesn't look a thing like a fire-furred hare," he protested, eyeing the results of the chase with a wary eye.

"Nor you a Prince of Ilsfacar," I added, more concerned with the condition of my companion than the quarry he had brought down. I have rarely seen Foo in such a state, and never so happy about it. He was filthy – his fur was damp in jagged patches and all of his leatherwork was soaked to a uniform dark brown. His tail had the look of tarred string, and his haunches were muddied right up to the hem of his tunic and probably beyond that. He'd dropped his cloak in his mad dash out of the window, of course, the hunter always preferring to be unencumbered on the chase, but the light autumn drizzle was no explanation for the state of him. The figure he had brought back with him was no better off, not least because the scanty silk and satin she was wearing was the most unsuitable garment for a rooftop chase that I could imagine. It might have been emerald green once, a match to her eyes, which regarded Kirby with wary sullenness and myself with clear alarm. She was one of those women who, being born to a harsh life, flower early and lose their beauty in childbirth; she was young, and her body was voluptuously attractive despite the mud and the torn clothing, but her face was already old before its time.

"No matter," Foo dismissed airily with a wave of his hand. "It was a good hunt, all the same. A merry dance she thought to lead me, under roofing stacks and guttering water spouts – as if I'd lose such a trail simply on the scent of water!" He grinned, flashing his exhausted prey a line of white teeth, and she flinched, misinterpreting his expression. "Did you think me no more than a paltry hound?" he wondered. She shook her head mutely, cowering away from him into the curve of Treacher's arm. "The roofs of this accursed street are a city unto themselves," he went on, staring down at himself as if he'd just realised the state he was in. "Draped in torn nets like ragged spider webs, and cobbled in straw and slate and shingles." He rubbed thoughtfully at his shoulder, then looked at his hand with some distaste. "Broken slates might make good weapons thrown edge on, if they have thought and not panic to back them." He laughed again, his almost silent laugh that chitters in the back of his throat. "Not that I was in any danger of an unexpected bruise," he said. "She couldn't hit the walls of Oscallon standing on the inner lake shore, let alone a true child of the Hunter."

Treacher sniggered, earning himself a frown from Kirby and a hurt look from his captive. I merely looked at my R'rruthren friend sceptically. The walls of Oscallon are protected by many things and I suspect that throwing stones at them might prove more dangerous than shying slates would ever be – no matter who you were throwing them at.

"I understand the water," Kirby said, transferring his frown from his officer to the victorious hunter, "but what about the rest of it? You look as if you took her dancing down the Gutter before you brought her here."

Foo's whiskers twitched with brief repugnance at the thought. "It might have been better if I had," he hissed. "Is there no ordinance 'gainst the keeping of pigs in your district, Captain? The residents of this street wall them in with muck and mire, up to their shoulders. We tumbled down a rickety stair and into the lower yards behind some buildings further down the street. I will not call them houses, for they were not fit for a Trog to live in."

"Sinkhole Terrace," Treacher identified with resignation. "The whole block should be pulled to the ground, but the owner lives in the High City and won't waste his money on the labour. It'll fall down one day – if it doesn't burn down first."

"Trogs aren't that picky," Kirby added wryly. "We ignore those we occasionally find sleeping in the sewer pipes. They keep the rats under control."

The woman shivered, and I couldn't blame her. I don't like Trogs either; they're nasty, vicious creatures whose only saving graces are their cowardice and their stupidity.

"Well," Foo went on, looking a little annoyed at the interruption, "there were no Trogs in this place – only pigs, squealing and raising a ruckus at being disturbed. I nearly lost her there – the scents were overwhelming – but she'd overrun herself and had no breath to make her escape. I brought her back along the main street, as you know. Once I had her," he flexed the claws on one hand, out and in again with an easy gesture, "she was no trouble at all."

"He had no right to be chasing of me," the woman accused sullenly. "I ain't done nothing."

"Then you had no need to run away," Kirby pointed out. "You were watching my mage at work, were you not? Why did you scream?"

She looked up at him, her eyes brimming with sudden tears. "And why shouldn't I scream, with the knife put in my man's guts a second time? That black-hearted whoreson promised him no harm if he coughed, and he did that, for certain. Bad enough to be short-shrifted by his supplier on the hill that night – and then he had to come round and demand his part of it!"

Kirby turned to look at me with a knowing glance. It confirmed a little of what we had suspected – that the dead man had known his killer, and that they had quarrelled over some questionable business. The mention of the 'hill' brought the beginnings of a frown to my face; the discovery of Reinwald's book – too sure a sign to be pure coincidence – had suggested that the victim might have been the thief I was looking for. "I think," I said softly, "that you had better tell us all you know."

She shrank back against the lieutenant's studded

shoulder and shook her head with hurried fear. "I will not," she denied. "He'll use me for drake bait if I tell on him."

"Not if we find him first," Kirby announced sternly. "Which we will, if you tell us who we will be looking for."

She shook her head again, terror written in her eyes. "I canna," she insisted. "You don't know what he's like ..."

"We will," I said. "If you tell us. Nothing will happen to you. I swear it. I will find this man and bring him to justice before he can harm you."

"You?" She laughed a little hysterically. "Fancy armour and noble words won't protect you from *him*. He'd eat you for breakfast."

Foo drew in a hiss of breath at the implied insult, while Kirby merely gave her a broad smile. "I doubt that, missy," he said, sharing the joke with Treacher, who grinned at me knowingly. "Or perhaps you do not know who has just offered you her protection?"

She shrugged in the lieutenant's grip. "You think I mix with the likes of her?" she questioned defensively. "Who cares that noble bitches like to play at men's games? It won't matter to *him*."

My faithful R'rruthren snarled at that, a deep throated sound that made her gasp and cower back in alarm. Kirby's smile became a frown, while Treacher looked distinctly worried. I, much to the surprise of all of them except perhaps Foo, who knows me only too well, simply laughed. "Wench," I said softly, stepping across to consider her more closely, "Fear may make you foolish, but even that is no excuse for being rude. Were I one of the Endor Elite I might have had your tongue for such an insult."

She flinched, but she lifted her chin defiantly. "You're neither tall, nor black of skin," she accused. "I know about those women warriors. One of *them* I might believe. But – but ..." She trailed off, her eyes resting on my throat where My Lady's stone sits like a point of diamond fire against my skin. I schooled my face back into its mask of impassivity, letting her consider the implications of what she had seen. "Is that ...?" she tried, the question dying into a strangled squeak. "Are you ...?"

I took pity on her confusion. "I," I offered gently, "am Parisan, Knight of the Diamond Circle and sworn servant of Our Lady of the Sighs. I have promised you my protection, and you will have it, by My Lady's name. And he will stand with me," I added, indicating Foo with the barest tilt of my head. She followed the line of it with wide eyes, and shivered as she looked back at me.

"Believe her, missy," Treacher advised gruffly. "This friend of yours won't match between the two of them, that's for sure. If he could, he wouldn't be keeping company with the likes of you or your man, I bet."

She glanced up at him, then across to Kirby's patient face before she nodded a slow acquiescence, slumping as if resigned to her fate. "It don't matter," she realised. "He'll look for me in any case, soon as he realises I must've been here. He's a demon if he's crossed."

"We're good at demons," Foo remarked casually, and this time it was Kirby who winced.

"It had better not be in my District," he muttered. "I still remember the last time."

Foo laughed, while the woman looked confused. I ignored both the confident comment and the captain's reaction to it. "What is your name?" I asked instead. She thought about it for a moment.

"Linell," she said eventually, then added, "Just Linell. Nothing else."

"That's a pretty name," Treacher said brightly, earning himself a second wince from Kirby and a withering glare from the woman he held.

"Well, Just Linell," I said kindly, "tell us the tale, and we will do our best to help you."

She turned her glare on me, the fire of it dying into doubt as she met my eyes. "You really promise?" she demanded. "You'll find him?"

"I promise."

She nodded, putting her hands together to wring them nervously. "I've no mind where to begin," she offered warily. "My man was Kerkle, and he was a lazy son of a she-drake. Rather take from someone than earn a crust the hard way – except he was good at the lifting, and he'd never been caught enough for it to matter. He never took much, you see – just enough for him to get by, and then for us, when we took up together. Took me out of the bawdy house, he did, and treated me kind," she added, her look challenging any of us to dispute the fact. "'Bout three months back he came in with a tale of drinking with moneyed folk, and how one of them was going to make him rich. I suppose this Swelm – him, you know? – he must've overheard him boasting, because he came and demanded a piece of it. Kerkle was scared of him, too, so he agreed to a partnership. He gave up with the lifting and they took to going up into the High City, late – just now and then – and they'd come back with bits and pieces, odd things, rings with bits of rock instead of jewels, and plaited bands of hair, and stuff like that. I didn't know what they were, but he said they'd sell. Swelm knew where, you see, and Kerkle – he knew the one who was passing them. Anyway, things were good for a while, even if he had to pass a cut back to the one on the hill, and then Swelm came round more often, accusing my man of holding back and saying there would be more to take if they just ignored the one slipping them the goods.

"Kerkle was agin that. He said as how it'd be dangerous to cross anyone with magic to hand, and Swelm always agreed in the end. He'd eye me up, you know? As if he wanted me too, but hadn't quite decided on the how of it yet. Kerkle used to fight with him over me, I think. Anyway he, my man that is, he took to shooing me out the window when *he* came round, because the business went better that way. I'd hide and listen to them talk about the man on the hill, and how they could milk him for more of the things.

"Then last night..." she hesitated in her tale, pausing to

brush at her cheek with the back of her hand and leaving a smudged streak of dirt behind. "Last night, Kerkle went up to the hill again, without telling *him* he were going. Said he wanted to make a special trip – said he was going to get enough to get us out of here and somewhere better for it. He talked about going down river to Moderain, or even on to Carthery. Said there were better opportunities for a man with his wits about him than could be found squatting by the Gutter. He was full of wild talk, I guess. The Velvet City would be no place to hide from Swelm Usurus – he came from there to begin with. And Moderain's not far enough. Teneris, I said, or even Oscallon. He wouldn't listen. Kissed me and went, whistling, as if all our troubles were ended.

"He came back roaring drunk. I didn't know how to take him then; angry he was, because that bastard on the Hill had answered to his knock, and there'd been no stuff to collect. Double crossed him, see. Didn't need him anymore, he said." Her eyes flashed with sudden fire as her tone conveyed exactly what she thought of that. "Nobody pulls that on my man. He waited and went in the place after the lights were out. Oh, the piece he lifted! Beautiful it was – like nothing I'd ever seen. Big enough to sit in my hand, and so full of light..." Her face, which had lit up at the memory of whatever she might be talking about, fell again into tight lines of distress. "Only *he* took it, didn't he? Came round this morning demanding his cut and wouldn't believe there weren't any of it. Demanded it, he did, and when my Kerkle ..." She broke off with a sob, turning to bury her face in Treacher's tunic.

"Damn him," she muttered, viciously. "We could have cut the piece and shared it. But he had to have it all, didn't he?" She turned back to me with a determined look. "You find him," she demanded. "You find Swelm Usurus, and you cut off his poisoned hands, and you stick his black heart, and may the gods chain his soul in hell to rot for a thousand years!"

I answered her anger with patience, neither agreeing

61

nor disagreeing to that hate-filled demand. After a moment, she slumped back against the officer behind her and sighed with resignation. "It won't bring him back, will it?" she decided. I shook my head.

"No. No, Linell, nothing can do that now. Not even My Lady can drag a man back from death once the gates have closed behind him. He would not thank you if you could recall him here in any case – he is beyond the judgement of the city now. But I will find this Usurus and bring him to justice. No man has the right to kill another over the possession of a jewel, no matter how bright it shines. The Star Diamond did not belong to your Kerkle, and he had no right to take it, but he had no need to die for doing so."

Her eyes were briefly suspicious. "I never said it was a diamond. How did you know that?"

Foo laughed. "Bless you, missy," he yawned, alarming her with his sudden array of dagger teeth. "She knows a great many things no-one ever tells her. But there's too much you haven't told us yet."

"True enough," Kirby frowned. "We know what this man looks like, and his name, but not much more. It's little to go on in this city of ours."

"We know a great deal more than that," I said, favouring Linell with sympathy. "We know he comes from Carthery, that he's been passing minor magic out into the market for three months now, that he favours his left hand over his right, and he has a reputation for violence. Besides," I went on, "it's not information we need to find him, merely something he has owned for long enough."

"A finding?" Kirby questioned, obviously not having considered the idea before. "Iglen might be strong enough for that – if we had anything to focus on, that is. It would have to be something pretty personal, too – those spells can be very unreliable." He frowned, first at me, and then Linell. "We don't have anything. He took more than he left behind."

I didn't laugh. The matter was deadly serious, and I

would have offended his sensibilities in any case. Kirby is a good warrior and a shrewd man but, like many of his kind he tends to think linearly, which is one of the reasons he is content to be a captain in the City Wards and not a general. "We have the perfect focus for a finding," I announced, deliberately not looking in Linell's direction as I did so. "He very kindly left it for us – although I doubt he would have done so if he'd realised it could be so used."

Foo, who had been frowning as deeply as Kirby still was, drew in a hiss of realisation. "Of course," he breathed. "What's more personal to a man like this Swelm than his knife?"

***

Iglen's face was paler than usual as he re-emerged from the depths of his bag. He was muttering – not carefully defined words of power, however, but uncomplimentary considerations of his company's ancestry. Kirby was carefully ignoring him, taking the opportunity to finalise the arrangements for the disposal of the body and Kerkle's personal effects. He'd sent Linell back to the watch house under armed guard, as much for show as for her protection, which had probably given the general population the distinct impression that she had been responsible for her lover's death. The hardest part of our whole arrangement had been convincing Iglen that he should cast the finding spell at all. He had a headache, he'd told us sourly, and the previous casting had left him drained and insensitive to the working of further power. Kirby flatly refused to believe either statement, which hadn't helped to make the mage agreeable, and it wasn't until I suggested that I deal with the headache before we began that Iglen had finally given way on the matter.

Foo had disappeared somewhere during the prolonged discussion, and only reappeared once everything was settled. I wondered where he'd found clean water to sluice the mud from his flanks, but refrained from raising the question, merely greeting him with an approving nod as he bounded down the outer staircase to rejoin me. His fur was still damp, but it was neatly combed into place and all his trappings were gleaming once again. Iglen looked up at his arrival, huffed, and bent back to his assembled bits and pieces. Like many a mage of his ability he relied a great deal on pre-prepared items for his bespelling, and I knew that much of his time back at the watch house involved long hours crafting possibilities rather than in further research and study. Some of the skill he brought to his position was an uncanny ability to have the right items stowed in his cavernous bag, and I had been certain he would have the makings of a finding spell somewhere to hand, even if we had not considered the need for one before we left the watch house. An Archmagus such as Reinwald might have constructed the enchantment with simple words and gestures, but then, even in Oscallon, magicians with that kind of power are rare. Iglen's fumbling with string and wax and coloured powders was messier, but we were looking for results, not elegance.

The Warders had dispersed the previously gathered crowd and, while I knew that many a curious eye would be watching us from half shuttered windows, there were only a few people still to be seen in the street. I had no difficulty in focusing my inner concentration, seeking the point of stillness that lay within me. Light flared briefly at my throat as My Lady answered my unvoiced prayer and I moved to Iglen's side to drop my hand softly to his shoulder. He looked up with irritation; then his face relaxed with surprise as my touch transferred the warmth I had requested. It was only a brief gifting of strength, but I knew it would be sufficient to banish a little of his fatigue. "Thank you," he said, finding me a simpering smile and a nervous twitch of his chin before ducking back to his work. This was about as gracious as Iglen can get, so I added my own silent thanks to My Lady and left him to finish his preparations. I found Foo watching me with a knowing grin.

"What will you do," he wondered softly as I moved to join him, "if one day she does not answer you?"

I frowned reproachfully at him. "I will know that what I asked was not intended," I replied sternly. "I serve her, not the other way around. She knows when there is need."

He accepted that with a sage nod of his head. "'Tis a pity she sees no need to aid you in the matter concerning Reinwald," he said.

"She may yet," I replied, "but right now I have a promise to fulfill. We have a murderer to find."

Foo's ears flicked. "I do not trust Iglen's strength after his last casting. We are as like to end up following flitter trails as we are finding our quarry."

"Have no fear of that." I bent to check the fastenings of my greaves. "My Lady's aid comes in many forms, and I have no doubt her hand guides me, even if you cannot recognise its touch, my friend." He tilted his head to one side, eyeing me with a questioning frown, and I smiled at his quizzical expression. "Think on it, oh mighty hunter – how it is we came upon the quarrel of the very men we seek?"

"We were looking for the Carthery connection," Foo said, not following my thought at all. "And found it, too, if the trollop's word is to be trusted, although I doubt that this Usurus is any threat to Alwick's diplomacy."

I nearly laughed at that, imagining how a truly suspicious politician might read recent events. "No," I agreed, checking that Dancer was secure at my hip and ensuring my purse was well settled beneath my breastplate. "Not even Octian's enemies would consider something so convoluted as kidnapping Broderick's tutor in order to disrupt the Royal Household. And if they had, they would have pursued it with more show than simple mystery. 'Tis possible the Duke himself might think of such a plan, but it is in his interests to make this meeting – not sabotage it. No, my friend, I suspect our plotting is less directed than that. Something more personal than politics. You know that I paused to seek guidance in the Chapel before we came here?"

"Aye – and got no answer for it." He was watching Iglen begin to lay out his powders in the street. I finished my checking and moved to sit beside him on the stairs.

"But I did."

His head swivelled to consider me in surprise. "I thought …?"

"I did not hear voices, or see signs," I agreed to his protest. "I rarely do. But what sent Bardoff to Kirby's office the very moment that we were leaving? And why else did Iglen insist that this minor dispute was worth the consideration of his captain? My Lady's hand is subtle."

He considered that, his eyes watching the mage at work, but his thoughts centred elsewhere. "I cannot quarrel with that," he said at last. "Although it might be the hand of Athnea who stirs us, not your own patron."

The possibility had not occurred to me, and I thought about it as Iglen lit a coloured candle in order to drop wax upon the cobblestones. Since my dedication to my Lady I have had little need to petition other powers in this world; I know who guides my footsteps as surely as I know the numbering of the days, but, unlike many of the priests of my faith I do not question that those other powers exist. I have seen the evidence of it, over and over, and understand that the gods are many and our comprehension of them incomplete. A wise man of my acquaintance once suggested that all gods were but aspects of a greater power, just as all days make up a greater year. If that were so, then serving one would be to serve them all. For myself I see them grouped as are our earthly rulers, each sure of their own people and working for their interests, much like Alwick and his diplomacy. It was not inconceivable then that my Lady might offer my service to aid another in the Celestial Ranks, nor that the Spinner of Fates might be persuaded to twist her thread for my Lady's aims. Since the outcome was the same whichever way you looked at it, it seemed impertinent to question the hows of its execution. I had prayed to my Lady for help in unravelling the mystery of Reinwald's disappearance, and soon thereafter

I had found myself in pursuit of his stolen diamond. I had no doubt that one was the result of the other, however it had been achieved.

"It's possible," I conceded. "Although if my life is woven through the Spinner's tapestries it was stitched there by my Lady's hand."

He laughed, softly. "Is that not true for all of us?" he asked. "I know my heart dances with Inlahin, and that in the end I shall meet the Hunter face to face. Yet my life is tangled up with yours, and thy goddess dictates the pattern of my dance while I remain at thy side. That was my choice, as much as you made yours."

"True enough," I said, favouring him with an affectionate look. "And I trust you never have cause to regret it."

"Oftentimes," he laughed, springing to his feet. "But never when the hunting is good. And today we hunt for certain!"

Iglen had completed his painstaking preparation. Usurus's knife lay in the centre of an elaborate pattern of wax and powder, Kerkle's blood a dark crust on its blade. Kirby was issuing orders with his usual succinctness. "Bardoff," he barked, "you stay here and get Iglen back to the watch house when he's finished."

"Which I will be," Iglen muttered with a sigh of martyrdom. His captain ignored him.

"You'd better come with us, Treacher. If this man is anything to match his reputation, an extra sword won't go amiss. Now – we will be going out of our District, by all that's likely, so don't step on any toes you shouldn't."

"No, sir," Treacher acknowledged, sharing a grin of anticipation with Foo as the R'rruthren stepped carefully into the spot that Iglen indicated he should. I followed him into the pattern, trying to avoid disturbing the careful work. Kirby was the last to take his place. He paused halfway there to glare at his watch-wizard with a moment of impatience.

"Iglen," he said pointedly, "I trust that blade is not going to fly through my streets point first? It's already killed once today. I don't want to lose our quarry because I'm busy pulling his knife from somebody else on the way."

Iglen frowned at him, then glanced down at the knife. A brief quiver of embarrassment shot across his face and his shoulders ducked as he shook with a sudden nervous giggle. He reached into the pattern and flipped the weapon over without a word, giggling again as he did so. Kirby sighed and stepped into place, while Treacher exchanged a knowing grin with Bardoff, who was trying hard not to laugh. I schooled my own face into impassive detachment. It wouldn't have been funny if Kirby hadn't noticed Iglen's mistake. Magic is tricky at the best of times, and the slightest slip of concentration or attention can have messy results, as Deckle's failure with his fire spell had clearly demonstrated. It is why the priests of my faith discourage its study and disapprove of its practitioners, arguing that men should not play with forces they cannot control. I happen to disagree with that argument, despite having had to deal with far more consequential results of mishandled magic than most: if men of true worth and wisdom do not master the powers of this world, then they will be left to those with fewer scruples and greater greed. Magic is not evil in itself and can be used for great good; it is the responsibility of those who wield it to do so. That some occasionally overreach themselves and fail does not condemn the many who do not – a point I often argue with my confessor, who regards the City of Oscallon and its web of magic-strewn streets to be as evil a place as Carthery.

Iglen resettled himself at the apex of the design, kneeling directly behind the recumbent knife, its hilt now pointing away from him. He was still pale, and I wondered if perhaps I had asked too much of him by requesting a second wreaking so soon after the last. It was far too late to change my mind. Arcane light spread out from between his fingers, following the lines of the pattern that enclosed us. It wove an intricate cage around the knife, which rose slowly from the cobbles to hang at the mage's eye level, suspended by nothing at all.

"Higher," Kirby hissed, risking breaking the man's concentration. "We shall lose it otherwise."

Iglen's eyes closed with effort and he lifted his hands as if they supported a great weight. The knife quivered, then reluctantly moved upwards. Inch by careful inch the cage of power pressed in upon the blade until it shimmered with the pale crimson light of Iglen's casting. The mage was swaying with exhaustion; he brought his hands together, battling the pressure that held them apart. I held my breath, my eyes fixed on the quivering blade that, by now, had absorbed all of the spell. Somewhere to my left Iglen threw his arms wide, releasing what he held with a gasp of effort before he slid, unresisting, to the ground. I had no time to learn whether he was unharmed by his work.

The knife, bound by word and power to seek its true master, had leapt forward, and the chase was on.

Chapter Six

Down Packers Street, along Salters Lane, past the Netmaker's well: the trail led through the twisted alleys of Gutterside, dodging this way and that as the finding sought the quickest and easiest way to its destination. The enchanted knife swerved around corners, indifferent to all but the most impassable of obstacles. We ran through narrow passages, leaping over abandoned boxes and kicking our way past unidentifiable rubbish. We swerved past loaded handcarts whose owners turned to gape at our passing, and ducked through broken fences, or scrambled over them as our quarry darted through without pause. Left past the Duck and Dancer, straight through Victory Square, down the clatter of steps that led to Lower Cork Street we raced on, the blade a steady height above the ground, its speed undaunted by the twisted route it pursued. Foo was ahead of us, leant forward in the easy lope of his kind, following the tortuous dance with open mouthed pleasure. Behind him I ran with a studied step, careful not to overreach my speed, intent on my companion's tail rather than the effort of glimpsing the darting movement that he hunted ahead of me. Kirby's bulk was at my heels, panting a little with the effort, while Treacher pounded in our wake, casting back the occasional apology as we startled passers-by.

We ran from shadowed recesses out into the pale autumn light and then back again, the fine drizzle of the day impacting in our faces as we crossed open squares or the wider streets. People scattered from our hunt, alerted by the sound of our footsteps or the alarm that preceded them. In places we accumulated a tag-tail of ragged urchins whooping and screaming in our wake until exhaustion or boredom dropped them behind again. We crossed the Gutter in a wild scramble, Foo leaping with abandon from one bank to the other, the rest of us squelching from muddied slope to muddied slope in his wake. The stream was narrow at that point, saving us a questionable passage through its noxious waters, but even so the air reeked of fish guts and sewage. There was no time for hesitation, and we raced on, back into the twisted streets, darting in and out of crooked passageways, the glint of the enchanted knife always ahead of us.

Our chase led down into Fishers' Drop, the long line of warehouses, netting sheds and docks that border the north of the river. We pounded through open buildings, Kirby swearing as the knife slid effortlessly through the hanging nets. After the first such encounter, which had Foo scrambling up the draping network and the rest of us stumbling in all directions in search of a way through, I drew Dancer from her scabbard and simply sliced an opening in each of the subsequent obstacles. Kirby cursed me as I did so, finding breath to complain at the cost to the city, while Treacher was left to call back apologies to the indignant netmen and their disconcerted customers.

The knife hesitated at the river's edge, then plunged across, leaving Foo howling on the dockside. The Medlure is over a hundred feet wide at its narrowest point in the city, and while a R'rruthren can swim if he needs to, the river was full of traffic. I grabbed his jerkin and dragged him down a tilt of wooden steps into the bob of a small boat, cutting at the anchoring ropes as I did so. Kirby had already spotted the craft and clambered aboard behind us, yelling at the startled boatman who stood in its bow.

"Row, damn you, row as if your life depended on it!"

The man took one look at the tumble of figures which had invaded his craft, at the glint of my armour and Dancer's drawn blade, and lunged for the oars without question. We drove forward away from the dock, leaving Treacher to leap after us and land in an undignified heap, nearly swamping the vessel as it wallowed under his weight. I rode the dip and undulation of the craft almost without thinking. My mind, and my eyes, were fixed on the skim of the bespelled blade as it shot over the water. It jinked and swerved around a high sided trader as it pulled out from the quay, causing consternation on the decks; then it reached the far bank of the river and started across the open spaces beyond.

The Medlure is one of Nemithia's main thoroughfares; it brings traffic across from Daberon and the east to join what comes down from Tenaris and Oscallon in the north, and it carries the commerce on through to Moderain and Carthery to the west. It is a slow and placid waterway for most of its length, and it drifts through the city with general unconcern, carrying laden barges, high sided trading sloops, private river boats, painted passenger craft, and a good many freshwater fishing vessels, with equal indifference. It slides in past the eastern watergate, cutting between the High City and the Guilds' quarter before it curves past the palace and the park. It is here, at the western side of Asconar's capital, that the river comes alive. We were leaving Fishers' Drop behind us, its long clutter of narrow wooden quays clustered with small boats and sturdy fishing skiffs. The north bank is, on the whole, given over to the city's stomach. Ahead of us was Waterdock with its low stone quays and the wider loading docks of the warehouses and wholesale markets they serve. The river's level only fluctuates with the seasons, lowest in high summer, highest in early spring, but even that necessitates high built banks and jutting quays designed to account for the shifting levels. In autumn the Medlure is neither high nor low. It rubs shoulders with the wooden support piles and the stone walls that contain it, the river's surface a good arm's reach below the line of the docks themselves. The knife had simply sped at head-height across the water and on, over stone flagged loading areas and into the district beyond.

We bumped ashore against a set of worn stone steps and Foo sprang lithely to the dock above. I followed, sheathing Dancer as I did so, my heels ringing sharply against the stone. Kirby barked at Treacher to pay the man and scrambled after us, cursing as he realised we may have lost our quarry.

"This way," Foo hissed, darting forward to disappear around a stack of casks and boxes. We pounded after him, breath and effort rested by the short respite over the water.

The trail was not as hard to follow as I'd feared. The docks were busy, a bustle of activity that shamed the huddled reluctance of Gutterside. Men were shifting goods, loading and unloading ships and wagons, while their masters haggled over prices or berated their inefficiencies. The passage of the knife had caused a stir of alarm, overturning a cart of grain and scattering the labourers who were stacking it. Foo bounded over the tumbled sacks, neatly avoiding the indignant merchant who grabbed at him. Kirby threw him a look of apology as he and I followed suit. Beyond we could just catch the glitter of the speeding knife as it jagged further into the maze of streets and storehouses.

On, then, through Waterdock and the loom of faceless buildings where counting houses and offices crowd between tight-packed warehouses and open stores. We thundered along streets paved with wagon rutted stone, passing the haggle of wholesalers and merchants, and avoiding the spill of commerce and trade that was busy ignoring the greyness of the day. Onlookers turned and gawked at our hunting, wary guardsmen grabbing at their sword hilts, portly overseers glaring with indignation. The cobbles were slicked with rain and we ran past figures who huddled around glowing braziers under dripping awnings. Still our guide hurtled onwards, turning sharply as it reached an internal city wall and speeding along its length. It circled the Festival Fountain once, then drove straight through the Purchase Gate. Foo swerved past the startled trader who was talking to the gate guard, ducked under his mule without missing his pace, and vanished into the confines of the Inner City. After a moment's alarmed confrontation with the guards, Kirby, Treacher and I followed.

If Fishers' Drop serves the city's stomach, the Inner City serves its soul. There are shrines elsewhere in Nemithia, but it is mostly in the Inner City that the gods are worshipped and acknowledged above all things. The district houses more than temples, of course – there are houses for the priests, the workshops of dedicated craftsmen, markets for the purchase of sacrifices, wine and other sacred intentions, and the normal spill of administration and other anonymous buildings all competing for space where they are able; but it is the temples that dominate the area, in more ways than one.

From the lowest worship pit of Val'Vachea to the tallest spire of the Celestial Watchers, the Inner City echoes with devotion to the higher powers. Unlike many of the Known Kingdoms, the people of Asconar are cosmopolitan about their gods and are not averse to petitioning several in pursuit of fortune or favour. There is no official religion as such, although the royal family pay dutiful attention to the rituals of the Earth Mother's year. The temples jostle against each other with amenable rivalry, each promising their own form of spiritual salvation, each with their own unique flavour on view. Some are stricter in their requirements than others, of course. My own following, that of the Inner Trinity, insists that all other gods be forsworn by those who choose its path. Our devotion must be intense, but for those who have true faith the rewards are unquestionable. Most of the cults ask such dedication only from their clergy, and the average citizens of Asconar choose the deity that best suits their purposes until they perceive the need for any other. Prudent men often patronise more than one cult as well as several temples and, as a result, the Inner City has no lacking in finery, whichever House or Temple you choose to enter.

It was mid afternoon by the time we stumbled through the Purchase Gate and past the patterned steps of the Temple of the Bargainer. The streets were not crowded, but they were populated. Cloaked and robed clerics moved among a cosmopolitan company: wealthy merchants, earnest craftsmen and armed warriors rubbed shoulders with harassed mothers and unruly children, well dressed women and dowdy labourers' wives. Beggars squatted on street corners, and stalls offered choice merchandise ready for those who wished to purchase offerings. The Inner City is never quiet; its ceremonies play out from dawn to dusk and then from dusk to dawn as each of its temples follows their prescribed rituals in strictest order. Many of those who walked its streets that day would be visitors to the city, come to watch and wonder at the marvels of the place; among them would also be the opportunists, the pickpockets and the hustlers, taking their chances and casting the occasional gift into the Temple of the Spinner so as not to chance their luck.

Our quarry twisted down the route from Purchase Gate to that same House of Fortune, passing the many-shrined street of the Hearoith and skirting the edge of the vast underground Earth Shrine. Its flight was slower in those streets, the enchantment beginning to falter – either the original spell was fading, or the influence of so many gods was adversely affecting the charm. The hunt was also slowing, even Foo's seemingly indefatigable pace feeling the effects of the chase. I could hear Kirby's breath rasping as he pounded behind me, and I had no air in my lungs to do more than touch the crystal at my throat as we passed the largest of the Seeker shrines: that of Our Father in Prosperity. Beyond that was an open square dotted with well attended stalls, and beyond that the carved and decorated edifice that housed the Temple of Earthly Athnea, Spinner of Fates, Mistress of Time, and Goddess of Luck. High on its roof, supported by ornate buttresses, stood the Inner City Watch Clock. Its single hand showed it to be halfway through the fourth watch of the afternoon.

There, in the bustle of the square, the enchanted knife slowed to a quivering halt. It tapped gently at the shoulder of a tall man dressed in black leathers, then clattered unceremoniously to the ground. The man turned, his dark profile a matching reality to the shadow we had witnessed earlier in the day, and saw us as we came to a breathless stop, not seven paces from his side. He looked down at the tumbled knife, then up at Kirby's victorious grin and cursed, turning on his heel and breaking into a run.

We split – Foo streaking sideways to intercept his flight, Treacher breaking in the other direction to forestall a similar bid on the other side. Kirby and I took a breath apiece and went after him, hands dropping to sword hilts as we moved. Swelm Usurus was an easier man to hunt than his knife. The crowd parted ahead of him with wary reaction, and they eddied in behind us with curious stares and mutterings of alarm. He ran straight ahead, heading for the temple steps, probably intending to lose us in its maze-like interior. The goddess of fortune was not smiling on him that day; as his feet hit the lowest step the doors at the top of the flight swung shut with a hollow clang. He cursed and turned, only to find our pursuit drawn too close to evade by simple speed alone. A glance to either side confirmed his suspicions of being trapped – he was firmly penned by our tactics, the ornately carved walls of the temple blocking every avenue of escape.

Every avenue bar one. Even as Kirby and I reached the lower step he twisted to his left and ran for the carved pillar that supported one side of the building's massive door lintel. The Temple of Earthly Athnea, unlike that of her Celestial counterpart, is squat and over-ornate. Every surface, both inside and out, is carved and patterned with intricate detail; statues of strange beasts – some real, some rumour – swarm along every ledge and into every cranny of its construction. Many of them are as old as the original stonework underneath, and time and the weather have worn off some of their fearsome edges, but they were cut deep, and the images remain clear. Their indented surfaces provide perfect handholds for a desperate man, and Usurus scrambled up the pillar as if his life depended on it.

Foo leapt after him, his claws raking long rents in the back of the fugitive's tunic, then dropped to the top step, dislodged by a well placed kick. He landed on his feet, then staggered back with a violent sneeze, followed by another, no less explosive. I clattered to a halt beside him, torn between our fleeing quarry and concern for my friend. Kirby stopped a little further back and called on the man to come down. His answer was an offensive gesture and a continued ascent.

"Bloodit," the captain cursed. "He could hide for hours up there. We'd never find him once it got dark."

"All that," Treacher panted, joining us, "for nothing."

"He'll come down," I started to say grimly, already contemplating the pattern of handholds and ledges the climber had assailed, when Foo sneezed again. It was loud and startling; the R'rruthren leaped backwards with a yowl of distress, shaking his head to banish yet another threatened explosion. I swallowed my words and turned to look at him in puzzlement. His reaction made no sense, since it was earthly magic that irritated his sensitive nose, not the spiritual kind; he'd never had any problem with Temples before. My first thought was that Usurus had cast some kind of enchantment behind him, but Foo's powerful sneezes spoke of mightier magic than the assassin should have been capable of using. At that moment we all heard the climber gasp with surprise and terror. I looked up, stepping back to get a better view of what had disturbed him. What I witnessed made my blood run cold.

At the top of the pillar, some twenty or thirty feet above the top step, were clustered a group of grinning stone gargoyles, batwings spread and long clawed fingers raised to rake the air. They formed part of a larger sculpture, crouching beneath the turn of the Eternal Wheel, ready to feast on the flesh of those cast down for trying to cheat Fate. They were well-worn by wind and rain, the stone of their faces streaked with pigeon droppings and lichen sprouting along their wing tops – and they were moving.

One of them had seized Usurus' lifted hand, dragging him away from his hold on the stone. Another was climbing down the other side of the pillar, reaching round to claw at the man's unprotected back. Their movements were slow and awkward, like old men who had sat too long in the same place: they eased from their seats with the crack of broken stone, precipitating a shower of dust and chips that impacted against their victim's face. The man screamed, dragging a knife from his belt to slash desperately at the stone hands that reached for him. He dangled out over our heads, kicking and twisting as he fought to be free of his unnatural attackers. The knife blade broke, clattering down among us and we paced back, helpless to interfere in the battle as yet more of the stone shapes moved down to tear at the man.

"Fate and favour," Treacher hissed in horror, an appeal to the goddess whose temple we faced. "I did not know this place was so protected!"

"It's not," I answered tightly, staring up at the uneven conflict. "This is earthly magic's doing, not divine intervention. And I don't think it's under much control."

A silence had fallen over the crowd behind us, heads turning in search of the cries of desperation that rang out over the square. I turned to Foo, who was breathing with careful deliberation, his nose twitching with disquiet. "If you have breath and speed left," I said, "then run and find us a mage with the power to dispel enchantment. Start with the House of Study – there may be a scholar with power at Magrix's Altar today. If not, go on to the Celestial Observatory, and then try the Halls of Incantation. And hurry!"

He nodded once before he sped away, a dark streak swallowed by the subdued autumn colours of the crowd. Above us Usurus was in trouble: stone hands dragged at the leather of his clothing and snatched at his limbs. He no longer had any hold on the supporting pillar. Instead he dangled by the reach of his arm, still firmly held by the leering figure above him. He cursed and swore as he kicked to be free, but neither words nor boot leather seemed to affect the ponderous advance of his attackers. Beside me Kirby grasped the hilt of his sword with impotent anger. Only a fool would try to climb up to aid the beleaguered man, and the captain was no fool. Even so he wanted to be doing something, just as I did.

The curses of the dangling figure turned to screams of pain; blood was dripping down to the coloured steps, blood torn from flailing limbs by stone claws. I heard a crunching sound, the sort made by a hound as his jaws close on bone, and then Usurus was no longer dangling, but falling, his left hand still twitching feebly in the hand of the gargoyle who had ripped it from his arm.

He hit the steps hard, his legs buckling under him with the crack of breaking bone. He was screaming, his mangled wrist painting blood across the ground as he struggled to rise. My instinct was to move towards him; Kirby held me back with a warning hand. I looked up where he indicated and swallowed a curse. The moving statues were following the man's descent in a slow purposeful crawl. One of them jumped, its stone wings briefly spread to no avail. It crashed to the ground beside the injured man, one bat wing cracking away under the impact, and one leg crumbling under it. The damage seemed to have little effect. It groped towards the distressed Usurus, seizing the twist of his knee. He screamed again, and I could stand no more. I sprang forward, Dancer light in my hand, and slashed at the creature's head.

Sparks flew at the impact of stone and steel. The blow sang through my sword arm, reverberating across my shoulders. The ponderous statue paused in its groping and looked up at me, blind carved eyes unmoving in its worn stone face. I had done no more than chipped the line of its cheek.

"Back!" Kirby roared. He stepped in beside me, the dark blue steel of his blade a blur of movement. I dodged back to avoid the line of the blow and watched as the impact sheared into the gargoyle's neck and sent the head tumbling from its shoulders. He'd had reason to name it

'Stonecutter.' It was likely forged to aid against the Stone Folk, whose hides are solid as granite and twice as hard to cut. Against steel or flesh the sword is just a normal blade, but it cuts through stone or scales like a sharp axe cuts wood. Not even the enchantment that had brought this stone to life could withstand the power of that blade. The gargoyle's head tipped over and back, rolling across the steps to impact against the carved doors with a loud crack.

The body kept moving. Kirby swore, limbering Stonecutter round for another blow, while I grabbed the injured man's shoulder and heaved him away from the groping hands. Treacher reached to help me, wincing as the figure moaned and protested at the movement. "Bind his arm," I commanded as we reached the far side of the sweeping top step. "We need him alive." The lieutenant nodded and I bounded back to join Kirby as he faced down the advance of the statues.

The damaged one had taken short work to disable. Its limbs lay scattered at the captain's feet, still groping feebly against the mosaic. The others had nearly reached the ground by now, an implacable flow of stone clinging to the carved pillar with creeping ease. Kirby paused to take a careful breath, and he and I exchanged a glance of comradeship, reassuring each other of our readiness. "Easy as a Black Velvet whore," he panted, the toll of our hunting clear in his words. "You keep them distracted, and I'll keep them down. Didn't I warn you about meddling in the affairs of mages? Look where it's got us now!"

I laughed at that, feeling a surge of strength shiver through me. The need for battle always fills me with power, part of the gift of my goddess. While it remains I feel little pain and do not tire, although I pay for it afterwards. I am the vessel of my Lady's hand and, although the true weapon of my calling was beyond my reach for this conflict, I am always inspired by her presence within me. I wished, briefly, for Dispiriter's strength in my hands, then dismissed the thought and concentrated on current need. There were six advancing creatures, a medley of carved faces and unfinished backs where they had dragged themselves from their mountings. Some were winged, some not. One had six limbs, another had jagged horns sprouting from its brows. They moved with deliberate gestures, ponderous but still deceptively fast, as their rapid descent had proved. They made no sound in their advance but the drag of stone against stone, a silent parody of the creatures they had been carved to represent.

They gathered at the foot of the pillar, blind heads swivelling this way and that, as if tasting the air about them. Someone called from the foot of the steps, and a shield slithered its way across the mosaic at my feet. I risked a brief glance in that direction. The crowd had moved well back, leaving an open space in front of the Temple, abandoning the stalls they had been intent upon before our arrival. A portly man who wore a dark blue tunic and a look of wary terror was backing towards the relative safety of Our Father's shrine. Figures moved on the steps there, clear above the heads of the crowd. My free hand scooped down to collect the protection of the shield and a wild smile found its place on my lips. Call upon the gods and they will answer you, although not always in the manner you expect.

"Carry him to Our Father," I called back to Treacher without turning my head. Athnea's priests have no skill in healing –they are required to trust to fate in all things – but the Seekers make a practice of it, dedicated as they are to the healing of the Wounds of the World. I heard the lieutenant grunt some sort of reply but had no time to make it out. Stone feet shuffled on the mosaic and then rushed forward, reaching past our guarded stance, trying to reach their quarry.

Battle is no place for thought, only action. I took the full weight of the first rush on my borrowed shield, deflecting their advance into milling confusion. Stonecutter whistled past my shoulder, impacting into the upsweep of a wing; splinters of grey stone rattled against my vambrace. A living enemy would have cried aloud at the force of that blow; these unnatural figures made no sound at all. They did have wits enough to realise we were formidable opponents. They shuffled back and lunged more warily, stone claws reaching to test our guard while wings were spread to batter at our defences. I twisted Dancer in my hand, weaving a blur of steel between myself and their advance, seeing the sparks fly as her edge struck home, only to be deflected away. Granite wings hammered into my shield, driving me back with unwilling steps. At my shoulder, Kirby grunted and swung his long sword round with studied intent. Another stone head tumbled to the steps; then I heard him curse.

Dancer jabbed down, striking at the groping arm that had seized his ankle. I leant forward and rammed the headless body with the weight of my shoulder behind the shield. It staggered back, tangling another of its brethren as it flailed for balance.

Jab and strike, dodge and dance; step by step we were driven back by the sheer weight of their advance. Treacher was well behind us now; our effort was to keep them on the steps so that they could not scatter round us into the square. My shield arm was growing numb with the constant batter of wing and stone arm upon the painted surface. Dancer cut a glittering path that did little damage, but all the same discouraged. Stonecutter whistled with deadly effect, but the arm that wielded it was tiring. The only sounds in our battle was the ringing impact of steel on stone and the effort-filled gasps of the Ward captain beside me.

We held for a little longer; then the stand became a struggle for survival. Kirby slipped as his foot went back for balance and found the drop of the last step instead. Stonecutter sliced a deep gouge in the mosaic as he fell. Stone feet rushed for the resulting gap in our defences and I leapt sideways to protect him, taking the full fury of the foremost on my shield arm. Something snapped. I felt a distant flare of protest along my arm, but the warmth of my protector still enwrapped me and I gave it no heed. I flung Dancer, point first, at the silent yammer of the carved figures, bending to scoop Stonecutter up instead. The blade felt awkward in my hand, its balance too heavy for my reach.

I concentrated on slicing feet, intent on slowing their progress as much as I could. Still I was battered back, down the last step to stand defiantly in front of Kirby's tumbled form. He pushed himself up, still dazed, his hand closing over Stonecutter's hilt with automatic reaction as I thrust it at him; then a stone arm groped for him and he roared with realisation, swinging the steel round to strike with angered force. I left him to it, charging back up that first wide step to scatter what remained of our foe; headless statues with broken wings, still heavy and dangerous, severed hands grasping at my feet as I passed.

I whistled for Dancer and she came, a quivering of cold steel that slid, hilt first, across the coloured mosaics. My hand reached down for her; something struck my shielded side and pushed – and I went down, unbalanced by the weight. My helm hit stone and stars danced in my eyes. I heard Kirby call out: it was oddly distant. Hands were groping at my legs. I tried to lift my shield arm and couldn't; it was pinned down by the full mass of the gargoyle clambering onto it. Dancer's hilt was in my hand, but I could not bring her to bear. Stone claws scrabbled at the buckled shield. I was looking at a faceless death, one wing cut through completely, its distorted torso supporting two sets of clawed arms. I turned my head as it reached for me, finding the inner calm of prayer, unafraid to meet the goddess to whom I had dedicated my life. Time slowed to a crawl. I felt the touch of broken stone against my helm …

… and was blinded by the sudden flare of light that engulfed me. Heat exploded all around, accompanied by the crack of shattering stone. The weight on my shield arm was abruptly lifted, only to be replaced by a rain of undirected blows. Chunks of rock dropped in undefined patterns, driving breath from my lungs. The presence of my Lady went out of me in a rush, leaving me cold and shivering. My arm hurt, my head spun. I could not breath, or even move, so cramped and broken did I feel. I lay on the mosaic, trying to draw breath, wondering at the miracle that had allowed me to live. Light footsteps sounded close by, and I rolled my head over to find a familiar face staring down at me with concern.

I managed a faint smile despite the effort it cost, bringing Foo's dark visage into focus with difficulty. "Well met," I gasped. "Do we prevail?"

Chapter Seven

We had indeed prevailed. Foo had found an Elemental Mage at prayer in the House of Study and had persuaded him to our cause with hurried words and desperate pleading. The Master's name was Keldor Yelth, a visitor from Oscallon, and more than a match for the stumbling stone. Earth was not, regrettably, his speciality – his mastery was of fire – but his skill was sufficient to wreak exact destruction on our attackers. The square was littered with exploded stone, some of which still burned from within.

Kirby was climbing to his feet as Foo helped me limp to his side. The captain's chain mail tunic was torn, the embroidered tabard ripped to shreds above it. He was breathing heavily, but his grin held triumph as well as relief. I had no reason to argue with that; our conflict had been a desperate one and he had acquitted himself well. "Are you hurt, friend?" I asked as we reached him. He shook his head in weary denial.

"Not to notice, thank Midras. But what of you? I thought you lost when they had you down."

"So did I," I answered, the world drifting around me. My head spun and my arm hurt. I leant on Foo's solicitous support and watched everything recede into the distance; I scarcely noticed when Kirby reached to lift me into his arms, although I may have protested at the need for it. Light and shadows danced around me, fringed with colour and filled with echoing voices, none of which made any sense. I heard Foo sing my name and felt myself being lowered to a firm surface; someone touched me, moving my injured arm so that pain flared along the length of it. I gasped and sank into swirling greyness.

Warmth woke me, a subtle comfort that spread outward from my throat to enfold every part of me. It drove pain away as it spread, banishing every sense of distress but leaving a dragging weariness behind it. I opened my eyes, only to be dazzled by the light that flared from the crystal that I wore. A shadowed figure leant over me, hands laid upon my shoulders, unseen lips moving in a familiar prayer.

"… hands that hold the soul, soothe the pains of the world. Let us drink of thy tears, Lady of the Sorrows; let us know thy care of us. We are nothing but dust beneath thy robe, yet thy son has given himself for us. Hear –"

"– our prayers," I whispered, joining in the litany. The voice did not falter in its words, but the hands at my shoulders tightened their grip a little. "Let us be worthy of the sacrifice. Let us repent of our pride and be deserving of thy expectations. In the name of the Father, the Lady, and her beloved Son; may they bless us, and keep us. Amen."

The light died, the hands lifted, and I was looking up into the face of Cardinal Hyatt, the foremost of my faith in the whole of Asconar. He smiled down at me with gentle reassurance, touching forehead, breast and lips in a gesture of blessing before he moved away. I would have risen to show my respect but another hand restrained me. I turned my head to find Foo crouched at my side, his eyes widening into deep circles as the candlelight reasserted itself.

"Be still," he hissed. "Your Lady has asked much of you. Do not give more than there is need."

I laughed, feeling more than a little light-headed. "What she takes, she gives back with love, my friend."

"Amen to that," Hyatt remarked, reappearing with a filled goblet that he passed to Foo with a smile. "And her love has healed your hurts with less cost than I expected. But you still pay the price of her presence, as do all the vessels of our faith. You must rest."

"As you wish, my lord." I sipped at the wine that Foo proffered, glad at the support of his hand behind my head. I was tired – bone tired, the drained and empty shell that the withdrawal of my Lady's strength always left me. The cardinal laughed softly.

"I am your servant, not your lord, Lady Parisan. You are chosen by Our Lady and carry her blessing."

"And you are the voice of Our Father in this land, and carry his authority," I answered promptly. It is an old argument between us, a disagreement of mutual respect that neither of us would presume to put to the test. Only the gods knew which of us might be worthier, and if Hyatt held me in awe, it was no less respect that I held for him.

"Then in his name, be still," he commanded with a smile. "You may rest quiet here."

I glanced around to determine where 'here' might be. I lay on a low frame bed in one of the lower chapels of the Shrine, surrounded by flickering candles and painted images of saintly deeds. Foo perched beside me on a narrow bench, pulled across from its normal place in an alcove.

"I would," I realised, sitting up as memory of recent events came flooding back, "if I had peace of mind to do so. How fares Kirby? And the cause of our pursuit?"

Hyatt's frown was so full of displeasure that I slid back to the couch that cradled me without a word of protest. He continued to frown until he was sure I would make no more effort to rise again, then he sighed. "The good captain I sent home to sleep and regain his strength – as you should," he added pointedly. "Alas, for all our prayers, the gods called Swelm Usurus to judgement soon after your victory. He died with the Spinner's name upon his lips, begging her to be merciful. I pray that she will."

"He was one for the Underwolf, that one," Foo growled and Hyatt's hands danced through the gesture of protection in automatic response. The R'rruthren feel no fear in mentioning the force of darkness that stalks among their gods – they perceive him as being part of the greater pattern and have no worry that speaking of him gives him power. I have no fear of Foo's Underwolf either, although I would not care to face him – he is a guardian of dark places, and holds his throne by right – but Hyatt and I know of other powers: the dark reflection of Our Father's light always seeks ways to steal that to which he has no claim, and the speaking of his name has a tendency to draw his attention.

"Perhaps," the cardinal allowed, his voice a little sad. "But that was no way for a man to die. A wielder of great power sought his death, and the manner of it was cruel and unconsidered. Had you not been there to stay their attack they would have fallen upon a helpless crowd, and innocent blood might have been spilt."

I wondered at that. We had no way to know whether Usurus' unseen enemy would have struck at him had we not found him in the crowd, but the power needed to stir such unnatural life would not have been small and there were few mages outside of Oscallon or Posmera who would think of wreaking such a spell at a moment's notice. Unless, of course, they had the aid of some ancient artifact to inspire the act. Such things do exist – Foo and I have encountered many strange things in our time together – but I have never heard of any that can be wielded without cost. Would anyone choose such a way to silence a single man?

"Did he say nothing else before he died?" I asked. Foo's whiskers twitched.

"He was delirious with pain when Treacher laid him down," Hyatt considered thoughtfully. "We spared him that, at least. His words made little sense to us." He paused, recalling the broken phrases with a sorrowed expression. Hyatt cares too much for his work and regrets any soul lost, whatever the reason. "'If he wanted it back, he'll never find it now,' I think he said, then – something about a Magpie, and a Linnet – or perhaps some other type of bird. He was cursing much of the time. Cursing the gods mostly – a pox on the Swordsman, and drakes devour the Mage – that sort of thing. He swore against the Spinner for closing her doors on him, but at the last he pleaded for her mercy. I pray she saw fit to offer it. We offered him the chalice, that he might receive Our Father's judgement, but he refused."

"I'm not surprised," I observed, not unkindly. Death is

no place to change your allegiances to the gods, unless they have a direct interest in your conversion. Hyatt, like his brothers, struggles to bring all that he can under Our Father's hand, but even he would have to admit that there were probably other powers with a stronger claim on Usurus's soul.

"Nor I," he sighed, then smiled. "You must rest, my lady. I will have a litter summoned to take you home, and you may stay here until it comes. I will leave you to do so." His hands moved again, this time in the gesture of benediction, and then he went, the soft slap of his sandals against stone the only sound he left behind.

I sighed, turning to consider my remaining company.

"He's right," Foo said promptly. "You should rest."

"Are you my friend, or my nursemaid?" I questioned, raising myself onto my elbow so that I could lift the half empty wine cup from his hand. His eyes were pits of emerald fire reflected in the candlelight, and his ears flicked forward with mild exasperation.

"Both, if I have to be," he retorted gently. "You have but one life to offer your Lady, and you should not abuse it."

"Nor will I – but I cannot sleep with empty questions rattling in my head, as you well know. This business of Broderick's has become one blind alley after another."

"That's true enough," he remarked, succumbing to a yawn that curled an acre of pink tongue inside a cavern of ivory daggers. "All that running, for so little return." His mouth dropped open in a panting grin. "But it was a good hunt, all the same."

We were alone, so I blessed him with a warm, if slightly wry, smile. Foo is rarely disheartened by poor rewards. He lives for the moment – the Dancer's creed – and can find positive virtues in the most discouraging of situations. "Maybe," I agreed, "but what good is a dead fox if you had need of a live rabbit?"

"More use than a fox at large," he retorted. "Since live foxes keep rabbits in their holes. What you need then is a ferret to flush them out again."

I leant back against the supporting pillow and breathed out a soft sigh. The analogy seemed hopeless, since the only 'rabbit' we had sought had been killed by the fox. Who had in turn been killed – although not by us, but by some unseen enemy who had wanted him dead at any price. That thought struck a chord of resonance at the back of my mind and I frowned, trying to pin it down. "We started this morning with a mystery," I considered slowly, watching the tell-tale flick of Foo's ears as he followed my words. "An absent Mage and a broken mirror. We followed that to a second – the Mage still absent, but his workshop rifled and a diamond missing along with the man. That led us to a third …"

"A dead thief and his frightened lover," Foo interjected.

" … and a still missing diamond," I pointed out, sure that was important somehow. "And that led us to a fourth, with a dead assassin, murdered by magic … Foo? Did Usurus still have the diamond? Did anyone find it on him?"

He shook his head, puzzlement surfacing in his eyes. "No," he realised with an indrawn hiss. "There was no sign of anything like that. But he did have a hundred crowns in his purse."

"A hundred – where would a man like that earn a hundred crowns? No – forget I asked that. It was payment for something, not honest wages." Relief washed through me. "This trail is not quite cold yet, my friend. Of our four puzzle pieces, two are still unplaced – Reinwald is still missing, and so is his Star Diamond. From the other two, we begin to glimpse a little of the picture."

"We do?" Foo unsheathed the claws of one hand and used it to comb out his whiskers, yawning as he did so.

"I see a trail of deceit that has led to murder," I announced grimly. "Maybe three murders, although I pray that the Archmagus may yet be unharmed."

"Wherever he might be," my companion added, stifling yet another yawn. I chose to ignore the less than subtle hint.

"We have evidence of a conspiracy, with a shadowed figure at either end. Someone in Reinwald's household stealing trinkets of magic in return for – money probably – and someone at the other end selling them. In between we have a dead thief, and his equally dead partner."

"Neither of whom is likely to tell us any more than they have," Foo said sarcastically. "I do not have the desire to speak to the dead, even if we could find a Summoner powerful enough to call them back. We couldn't trust their word in any case."

I threw him a wry look. "Thurstan Rawnsley might command either spirit to the truth."

He hissed and spat at the suggestion. "You may choose to deal with the Black Crow," he yowled, "but your Lady would not like it. It was bad enough the last time."

I feigned unconcern, amused by his reaction. "But the College in Oscallon owes us over that matter," I said. "Rawnsley in particular. He does have the power to command those from beyond this world…"

Foo shivered, his tail quivering in rigid distaste. "Demons and devils are treacherous, and those who call upon them play with fire. As for speaking to the dead …"

I put out my hand and stayed his indignation with a reassuring touch. "Oscallon is several day's journey hence," I told him. "And I think this problem needs unravelling long before that. I am joking," I added as his wary frown failed to abate. "Rawnsley would not expend his efforts merely to speak to a thief, dead or not. He converses with those who can move mountains, and it takes a year or more to be sure of the task. You know I would not seek such a solution, except in desperate circumstances. Rest easy. I have no intention of disturbing the dead over this matter."

He sniffed and pretended to become intensely interested in his tail. I should not tease him over such things, but his reaction was so predictable that I could not resist the opportunity. Foo has no love for Thurstan Rawnsley, who once called upon us for help in a matter of some desperation. It is not easy to mortally offend a R'rruthren, but the man managed it somehow, despite being on the whole a rather pleasant character. I have no particular liking for his craft which, as Foo rightly said, is akin to playing with fire, but I respect his mastery of it.

Foo's original suggestion had not been intended seriously in any case. My Lady has given me power to restore the natural orders of life and death, not to disrupt them. I deal too often with the results of such meddling to consider it myself. Kerkle and his partner were out of my reach, and I had to concern myself with the slender threads they had left behind them.

"Perhaps I should sleep on it," I decided, realising that my thoughts were getting me nowhere.

Foo's ears perked up immediately. "I shall go in search of that litter," he said, bounding to his feet. "Don't move until I come back."

I didn't. I scarcely moved when he did return, except to sink into the summoned litter and direct the bearers back to Kellmarch House. I don't usually make use of the small, wheeled litters that ply the streets of the city, preferring to walk or ride under my own control. But they are sometimes useful, and I was grateful for them that evening, my armour hanging on me like lead and my limbs equally heavy. Foo laid his cloak over me for extra warmth, then clambered to the canopied roof and balanced there, untouched by the bone shaking rattle of our progress. I suspect he huddled in against the bite of the wind, and perhaps it was his predatory crouch that encouraged the bearers; they kept to a fast pace and did not pause once. The servants of the shrine had prepaid them; they hurried away once I had disembarked, in search of more lively passengers.

I stumbled to my bed, waving away Garrick's suggestion of food, but grateful for Delph's help with my armour. I wondered as I sank into the welcoming sheets just how close I had come to death that day: mere battle does not leave me so drained, nor simple healing either. In the many years in which I have served as my Lady's hand I have felt the surety of her touch more often than I would care to recall, and she never takes what she does not need, nor gives what is not required. It may have been that Hyatt's calling upon her for the aid of Usurus had touched me also, or else the impact of my skull upon the stone had done more than simply rattle my brains. Whatever the reason, I was drained to the core and, when I let it, slumber came quickly. My dreams were disjointed images of figures in shadow, of hands reaching out over the city. At the last the silhouette of a man held out his arms to me, his right wrist empty of a hand. Blind eyed gargoyles groped at the figure's feet, and then he turned away, leaving the vague impression of a second man, robed and bearded, walking among a scattering of stars.

I woke with the mage's name on my lips, and my cry brought Delph in from the outer room, his young face alarmed.

"Are you all right, my lady? You called out …"

"It was nothing," I assured him, sitting up as I did so. "What watch is it?"

"Ninth, my lady. Master Garrick said not to disturb you unless there was real need."

I glanced out of my window, to find the sky vaguely blue and the day relatively bright for autumn. "He was quite right," I said with a yawn. "Fetch me some hot kafir, will you? I must rise."

He nodded, his smile a little relieved. "I have polished your armour my lady, but your helm was badly dented. Master Garrick said to tell you he will attend to it today."

I acknowledged that with a smile of my own. "Thank Garrick for me, will you? And ask Foo to step up, if he's in?"

He dipped his head and left with eager steps. By the time he returned I had dressed in shirt and breeches and was in my outer chamber busy brushing out my hair. Foo was a bound behind him, snagging a cup of kafir off the tray the youngster carried as he passed. Delph placed the second cup within my reach, its top a creamy foam sprinkled with a pinch or two of crushed honey cake. "Has Garrick decided to spoil me?" I asked, "or is it just Bej in a good mood today?"

Delph grinned. Bej is the cook at Kellmarch house, a dour and taciturn individual whose love of food is only equalled by his apparent dislike of those who eat it. People usually complicate matters, and he prefers his life to be simple and uncluttered – unlike his kitchen, which is a veritable dragon's hoard of delights and secrets. Those who know him suspect that his surly attitude is merely cover for an over warm heart, but proving it would be a task beyond a saint.

"The words 'good' and 'mood' do not fit together in Bej's vocabulary," Foo considered philosophically, curling into the padded window seat and sipping carefully at his cup. Delph's grin widened even further.

"It was Master Garrick suggested the cream, my lady, but it were Bej who stomped over with the honeycake. He said if we were fool enough to waste good ingredients on a cup of kafir then we might as well do it properly."

I might have hidden a smile behind my cup as I tasted the concoction. The kafir was piping hot and warming, and the hint of honey eased the slightly bitter aftertaste. "Well, thank them both," I decided. "And thank you, Delph. Are you studying today?"

He grimaced but nodded an easy agreement. "Master Hoblan said something about maps, my lady. Will you be in for visitors?"

"No." I shook my head, picking up a silver clasp and reaching to gather my hair back into its usual tight confines. "Foo and I will be out. We have a number of people to visit."

'We do?' Foo mouthed at me from behind the boy's head.

"Would you carry a message for me before you attend to Hoblan's maps?" I continued, pretending I hadn't noticed the unspoken question.

"Of course, my lady."

"Good. Go to Lord Jarman in the palace and tell him to

tell his highness that our business is not yet completed, but I am attending to it. Don't linger in the guard house, whatever the temptation, and come straight back when you are done."

"At once, my lady." He bobbed his head and shoulders and hurried out, the tray dangling from his hand.

"Was that wise?" Foo asked, wiping cream from his upper lips with the back of his hand and then licking that away with a flick of his tongue. "Sending to Broderick, I mean? We are no further in this matter of Reinwald than we were yesterday."

"Yes, and yes we are," I answered, sipping at my kafir with appreciation. "Prince Broderick has commissioned us and has a right to know our progress."

"What progress? We found a dead thief, watched his murderer murdered and have no trail onward. All that happened yesterday was that you were nearly killed trying to preserve a man who'd have sold his own mother if there were profit in it." His mouth dropped in a silent laugh. "It was good hunting, was it not?"

"It was." I emptied the last of my drink, and leant back in my chosen chair. "And it drove our quarry out of cover, my friend. Don't you think it a little odd that someone should go to so much trouble just to eliminate one man? Those statues did not move by themselves. It took power to give them life – power and effort, I would say. Who would want a thief dead so badly?"

He shrugged. "The man probably had a lot of enemies. He was that type."

"That's true," I agreed. "But if Usurus had an old enemy that powerful he would have been dead a long time since. Whoever chose to strike at him in that manner had a recent grudge, of that you can be certain."

"So?" Foo shrugged a second time. "What does that prove?"

"I dislike the weight of co-incidence in this," I said, getting to my feet with determination. "Consider what we know. Someone in Reinwald's household was stealing minor magics and selling them on to Kerkle –"

"– who passed them to Usurus." Foo stepped down from the window seat with a sinuous stretch to help me buckle on my greaves.

"Who sold them to someone else, and the resultant money was split three ways. Only the night before last, Kerkle tried to break the pattern and went alone to his supplier …"

"… who didn't want to know anymore. Why not?" my companion wondered. "Had Reinwald found out?"

I shook my head. That didn't sound right somehow. "No – I don't think so. He'd have dismissed whoever it was on the spot – or worse, I should think. But Reinwald's disappearance is in this somewhere. Perhaps our unknown member of this conspiracy had already dealt with his master … No." I suddenly saw the picture, and it tumbled a number of things neatly into place. "Not had dealt with – but was about to …"

"So Kerkle was sent away empty handed," Foo was still wrestling with that side of things. "And came back to help himself. Which he did, because Reinwald was gone, and the wards were down. That still doesn't tell us anything new."

"Perhaps not, my friend. But it does show us the timing of it. I think we have ignored the motivations in this matter. Why would anyone risk Reinwald's wrath by stealing from under his nose?"

"For the money," Foo stated, as if that were so obvious it didn't deserve mentioning.

"Yes," I agreed, "exactly. So what did Reinwald have that was really worth stealing?"

He frowned. "Magic aplenty, I suppose. Who knows what an Archmagus keeps about himself? I'd have gone for the cash," he decided after a moment. "Less risky than magic, and easier to profit on. Gold, silver…" His eyes widened in realisation. "Diamonds!"

"My thought precisely." I buckled the last silver buckle on my vambraces and reached for my belt, letting Dancer's weight drape in her accustomed place on my hip. "But Reinwald would surely notice if the Star

Diamond went missing, so our would-be thief had to plan the matter carefully. He found a way to make his Master vanish and then…"

"Kerkle slipped in and stole the very piece he was after, right from under his nose!" Foo started to laugh. "A moment worthy of the Dancer, that. Thieves stealing from thieves."

"And two dead men to show for it," I reminded him, sternly. "No coincidence, Foo. Magic was wrought against Usurus by our unknown thief. Magic stolen from his master, I should think. I had a sense its wreaking was not entirely under control yesterday."

"But Usurus no longer had the diamond." Foo's objection was puzzled. He moved back to the window seat and sat on its edge, his tail flicked under him. "And where does all this take us?"

"Two places," I decided. "Firstly to Reinwald's house, to ask if any there remembers Kerkle, and then back to friend Kirby to make a linnet sing."

His whiskers curved down into a frown of confusion. "But the villain of this piece is one of Reinwald's people," he said. "He won't admit to knowing anybody."

"No, but I have a mind to read people's faces when I tell them of yesterday's events. Certain of yesterday's events," I corrected as thoughts tumbled into place. "Such as how Usurus was taken to the shrine of Our Father, but not necessarily that he died there…"

Foo's frown deepened into one of disapproval. "Whoever this man might be – or woman for that matter – they had the power to move stone into life. We may be stirring something worse than fire."

"Perhaps," I allowed. "But you and I should be used to that by now."

His whiskers twitched in wry reaction. He started to speak, but was interrupted by the reappearance of Delph, who knocked discretely at the half open door before he entered.

"Your pardon, my lady," he announced, "but there is a herald, sent to see you."

Foo and I exchanged a glance of surprise. "Lord Jarman?" I queried.

Delph shook his head. "No, my lady. The Lord Kembrian."

***

Kembrian is an angular man with a severe face and a starchy manner. He is also one of the King's personal heralds, holder of the title Master of Protocols, only second in rank among his calling to Lythian himself. This, in itself, was no indicator of the message that awaited me, although it did tell me from whom it came. Alwick sends personal messages only through the select few that he trusts to carry them – not a belittlement of his heralds' abilities, merely a wish to restrict those who are privy to his unguarded moments. The king of Asconar is an adroit politician, diplomatic to an extreme, capable of silken words and more than able to soften the hardest of blows where necessary. He can also be blunt, distressingly honest, toweringly commanding, and impatient with foolishness. That he manages to reconcile these two facets of his character, keeping his public face stern but fair, his private one robust and direct, is one of the reasons that makes him a worthy king in everyone's eyes – even those of his enemies.

You do not keep Alwick waiting. I rose to my feet and went to meet Kembrian at once, Foo trailing behind me, his tail twitching with curiosity. Delph ushered us in to the main chamber in our tower, announcing me with practised polish – The Lady Parisan, Baroness of Orandy, Knight of the Diamond Circle and Sworn Paladin to Our Lady of the Sighs – and the Herald rose to his feet from the chair he had appropriated and offered me the bow appropriate to my rank and position.

"My lady," he acknowledged. I dipped my head in return and waved him back to his seat.

"Kembrian," I said, managing to sound both cold and welcoming at the same time. I am never entirely sure if the man likes me or not. He is certainly not one to fear me, unlike many I could name at court, and he always gives the impression of being vaguely disapproving of me while being downright outraged by my choice of company. Protocol and the layers of respect and rank that surround it is Kembrian's entire life. I do not fit neatly in any of the categories that his tidy mind insists upon. I am a lady of some rank among the nobility of Asconar, and yet also a knight of no small renown; I keep the company of a R'rruthren Firstborn who lacks both title and official standing among his people, and I habitually move from High Court to common streets and back again without attendants or lackeys impeding my progress in either direction. He must despair of me as often as he does of Alwick himself – although never to our faces, I hasten to add.

"Is this a personal, or an official visit?" I asked, dismissing Delph to complete his assigned task and taking the chair on the opposite side of the fire. Kembrian bristled a little at the idea of him needing to seek my aid on a personal matter and pointedly laid his baton of office across his knees, as if to reinforce the weight of officialdom he carried.

"I am sent, my lady, with word from His Majesty."

"Which is?" I prompted mildly. The herald frowned a little, an indication of distaste for the manner of his message rather than its portent, since Kembrian is well schooled in his craft and heralds make no judgements on content. Composition, perhaps, but never content.

"I want to see you – now," was the short answer to my question, the message delivered in a polite interpretation of Alwick's bluff tones. It was a stark contrast to Jarman's message the previous day.

"Just that?"

"Just that, my lady. His Majesty gave no indication as to why he desired your attendance."

Somewhere behind me Foo growled something in his native tongue, a quiet comment I did not entirely catch. Kembrian threw him a disapproving look; he equates my companion's presence with Delph and Garrick's loyal attendance, and does not deem any servant to have the right to speak openly before his betters. I frowned in return, since I consider that particular assumption both ignorant and unworthy of a trained herald. The R'rruthren are not as we are. Their tribal standings and customs do not fit neatly into our society of ordered rank and precedence, where birth plays a vital part in the determination of respect. Foo may be Firstborn, and therefore unlikely to hold any office or command within his tribe, but he is a Free Hunter and nobody's servant – least of all mine.

"I will be with His Majesty within the watch," I promised, knowing that, without pressing reasons, it was unwise to ignore such a summons. Kembrian nodded his satisfaction with that and rose to leave. At the door he hesitated, turning back to me with an uncharacteristic reticence.

"I am told you were conveyed a message by young Lord Jarman yesterday," he said, trying to make the question sound casual and not quite succeeding.

"I was."

"Did he… acquit himself well?"

I wondered at the reason for the question but saw no justification in any response but honesty. "He did indeed. The youth has the makings of a fine herald in him."

Kembrian's tense expression relaxed with relief. "Indeed he has," he agreed with equally uncharacteristic warmth. "He is my sister's son, you know."

I didn't, but my impression of him softened in the light of that explanation. It was good to see that even the Master of Protocols possessed a more human side after all. "Then commend him to her for me," I said politely. "And to the Duke Lythian."

He acknowledged my words with a dip of his head, followed it with a deeper bow and left, leaving me to wonder just what Alwick wanted of me.

***

102

I took a moment to seek My Lady's peace before we left. My personal chapel lies at the very top of Kellmarch house, under the tiled roof of my tower. It is a place of quiet and contemplation, a chamber built from mellowed stone and filled with light during the day. Arched windows parade around the chamber, a curve of clear glass through which the sunlight is focused on my altar. There are no rugs upon the flagged floor, no hangings on the pale walls; its only decoration are the wrought curves of floor-standing candelabra and the silver twist of the triple cross that stands behind the altar stone. Some of my faith burden their sacred places with painted images and icons, draping their altars with embroidered cloth and laying jewelled pieces in praise of the Trinity. There is none of that in my quiet chamber. The pale stone is the only witness to the power of my Lady that gathers there; her presence is very strong, and needs no images to remind me of her sorrowed smile. The altar cloth is simple white. On it stands Our Father's chalice, which is filled with scarlet wine, the blood of his beloved son. Next to that is the silvered bowl filled with salt water, which echoes My Lady's tears.

Before them both lies my destiny and my dedication: the simple shape of my holy blade, both sword and sacred trust. Dispiriter rests upon My Lady's altar, filling the chamber with her presence and serving as a focus for my prayers. In truth, it is the sword that is the altar, not the cold stone that bears it, the silvered surface of her blade reflecting only truth, never illusion. The triple crossed pattern of her hilt is her only decoration. There are no runes scrawled across her steel, no jewels set in her pommel to flash or bedazzle the eye; she is wrought from a single length of what seems to be silver steel, and she shines with her own light, the barest shimmer of the power that sleeps within her.

I knelt before the altar and emptied my mind of all concerns. My prayers were those of thanks for my own deliverance, and hope for all those called to judgement in the day now passed. I prayed for Kerkle, and for Usurus, and I prayed for Reinwald, wherever he might be. A sense of peace settled over me, as it always does in that place. I would have lingered, but the world called, and I rose reluctantly, pausing only to lay my hand on Dispiriter's hilt before I left.

The binding beneath my fingers was warm, silk smooth and shaped exactly for my hand. No other soul in the whole of the Known Kingdoms can wield her safely; few can even touch her, since the strength of her righteousness burns like fire. Her kiss is final, and her judgement concise. Every day I present my soul for consideration, and every day so far she has accepted my touch. One day she may reject me; I pray that that day never comes.

Chapter Eight

I am no stranger to palaces, whether it be the brooding
halls in the depths of Zarh'ndani, the windswept
walkways of Vair Balessus, or the arching spires of the
High Towers in Oscallon. The Athel Palace in Nemithia,
ancestral home of the Kings of Asconar and centre for the
Royal Court in all bar the midsummer months of the year,
is one which has welcomed me many times over the
years. I choose not to live within its encompassing walls,
for my calling is such that I must be free to answer to any
who come seeking my aid. This is not unknown even
among the more permanent members of the court – the
palace maintains a fluctuating population of visiting
nobles and dignitaries whose constant comings and
goings tend to dictate that all but the king's own seek
their privacy elsewhere within the city. Reinwald was
one such, of course. Tutor to the royal princes and
advisor to the court, he nevertheless maintained his
household away from the bustle of the palace. I half
wished, as I made my way to one of the many palace
gates, that he had chosen otherwise. Few thieves even
chanced entry to the Athel Palace, and fewer escaped it,
despite the traffic that passed between court and city
during the day.

The black garbed Ravens on duty at the gate saluted me
as I passed. Like the King's Lions, they are sworn to
serve in constant duty to their monarch, and they take
great pride in their dedication. They are the guardians of
the palace and those its walls protect; by long tradition
commoners, rather than the Lions' noble lineages, but
steadfast and honoured all the same. I returned the
compliment with a salute of my own and entered the
citadel within the city, Foo bounding at my heels.

The Athel Palace is a vast sprawling complex with a
myriad of internal courtyards and buildings, all linked by

endless passageways and arches. At its centre rises the ancient keep that the Karhad raised for Finael, first King of Asconar, many years ago. The Ring Keep, it is called, from the shape it makes: one large fat tower bisected by a smaller one, like a stone set in a finger ring. The palace grew out of that early beginning. The vaulted halls that hold the stately court functions, the towers and their supporting complexes are all grafted onto that imposing edifice. Within the keep lie the private rooms of the king and his household, although the elder princes have long since chosen other wings of the palace to make their own when they are in residence. The heart of the keep, and therefore the heart of the palace and – by definition – the heart of both city and country beyond, is the throne room itself, wherein the King's Lions keep constant vigil over the symbols of our sovereignty; the crown of Fineal and the sceptre that bears the burning Eye of Concord.

Our steps took us in that direction, past the gilded arches of the Festival Hall and through the carved gates of the Tribute Arch. Black-clad Ravens stood vigil along the way, the birds they were named after squabbling over titbits at their feet. Courtiers and attendants scurried between the buildings, huddled down against the bite of the autumn wind, while the occasional scramble of children erupted across the courtyards, dogs and servants barking at their heels. Foo hissed at a loping wolfhound that ventured too close, and it turned tail and ran, leaving him laughing at its progress.

The Diamond Arch is the main entrance to the Ring Keep, a cascade of shallow steps leading up to a wide portico and the impressive metal bound doors of oak that are only ever closed in times of war. They were open, of course, flanked by matching pairs of Ravens and Lions, the king's own always taking that duty when their monarch is in residence. We were one of several groups of figures that assailed the steps, part of the normal traffic that spilled out from the Kingdom's heart. Even so, like the Ravens at the outer gate, the attentive guards saluted me, the Ravens with formal meticulousness, the Lions with a more casual acknowledgement of equality. I saluted them back as I passed, while Foo swept them an elegant bow that turned into a complete flip, his clawed feet landing easily in pace with my steps. I frowned at him as we passed under the archway, more through stern affection than disapproval, and he grinned back, unfazed by place or circumstance.

Once past the panelled hallway that lies beyond the arch, we reached the inner doorway that led into the larger tower and the throne room beyond. Here I paused to question the liveried footman who stood waiting to direct visitors. His answer turned us away from the flow of visiting traffic and towards a smaller doorway that lay to one side. One of the Lions was on duty there – a young knight wearing his newly-won mantle with pride. He drew smartly to attention as I approached, dipping his head in respectful greeting. "Be welcome, my lady," he said, reaching to open the door behind him. "His Majesty is expecting you. Go straight up."

"Thank you, Sir Richar." I acknowledged his greeting with the barest bow, then turned to glance at my companion. "Foo too?"

Richar nodded, grinning a little behind his sparsity of beard. In time, no doubt, it would match the magnificence of his father's, a generous bushel of ginger that the older knight wore with pride, but for now the young man's face was only brushed with a soft curl of down that added to rather than distracted from the bloom of his youth. "I have orders to pass you both, my lady. Lord Kembrian was most precise."

"He would be," Foo remarked irreverently. Richar swallowed a reactive snigger and waved us through.

Beyond the doorway was a spiral staircase and at the top of that a liveried servant who bowed deeply at my arrival, took our cloaks and led the way into the labyrinthine passages of the keep. We needed no guide, for I know the way to the king's private chambers well enough, but the man would have been offended had I even suggested there was no need of him. There is a

great pride associated with the right to wait on the king,
and the royal lackeys are as zealous in their attendances
as the Ravens or the Lions in theirs.   There are those
among the court who make the mistake of treating the
servants as if they are invisible and of no import, a
mistake Alwick is always at pains not to make. I know
well enough that if it is the lords who order the Kingdom
according to the king's law, then it is those in livery who
order the palace and the royal household at the queen's
desire.   Woe betide anyone who thinks to make it
otherwise; the royal staff know who they serve well
enough and their loyalty is generally above reproach.

***

Alwick Ravenlion, fourth king of that name in Asconar,
protector of the crown and beloved of his people, was
pacing up and down his study floor like a caged tiger.
His wife, the gracious Sharasaan, sat in a well-stuffed
easy chair working unconcernedly on an embroidery
while two white lion cubs tumbled under her feet. The
King looked up as I entered, the servant announcing my
arrival with authoritative tones, harumphed, and
dismissed our guide with a distracted wave of his hand. I
greeted him with my usual bow, while Foo dropped to a
crouch at my feet. Alwick stood and studied the pair of
us, a frown written across his genial features.

The King of Asconar is a bear in human skin, a
broadly-built man with a tumble of dark hair and beard
that, despite its spattering of silver grey, still frames his
face with determination. He is tall, too; a match to
Kirby's height but more solid in his bones, so that the
Watch Captain would have seemed slender next to him.
For all that, he is light on his feet and as agile as a cat –
as a R'rruthren, almost – and he is a superb warrior, his
swordsmanship honed on the battlefield as well as the
practice courts. He has a truly kingly presence – a
natural aura, not something of his own making – and it
would be hard to ignore him anywhere. Holding court he

108

is the focus of everyone's attention, and even here, in his private chambers, dressed in a simple embroidered doublet rather than the royal robes, he dominated the room without effort or even intent.

"Your Majesty sent for me," I said softly, trying to adjudge his mood. He was concerned about something, that much was sure.

"Yes," he rumbled, glancing at his wife as he did so. "Have you found Reinwald yet?"

The question startled me, since I was not expecting it, but I schooled the reaction from my face with the ease of long practice. "No, Your Highness. I have not."

"Bloodit," he muttered, striding across to sink into another of the well stuffed chairs. "Confound the man."

Sharasaan laughed softly. "Please," she said with graciousness, "both of you – sit and be comfortable. We have things to discuss."

"I have things to discuss," Alwick butted in, reaching for a goblet on the nearby table. He gestured to the chair closest to the fire and I moved across to join him, relaxing a little at being addressed with such familiarity. Foo loped after me, and one of the lion cubs hissed at his passing – a growl of friendly challenge, which he returned in kind. The cub looked distinctly startled and retreated behind its mistress' skirts, making the queen smile at the exchange.

"Does my lord wish me to go?" she enquired sweetly, placing her work to one side and reaching to gather her skirts. Alwick threw her an affectionate frown.

"No," he decided with warm exasperation. "He's your son too. And you know all about the trip to Hawksley, so don't pretend otherwise."

"No, my lord," she agreed, releasing the skirt and sitting back in her chair. Where Alwick is bluff and forthright, Sharasaan is elegance and dignity personified, an odd match to those who know neither them nor their history. She is his second wife, the first having died while birthing the Crown Prince, but she is held in no less regard because of that. Her ebony skin enhances her beauty; like many of the Endorian race she has retained a sense of youth with her passing years and her inner energies shine through with quiet confidence. The Queen of Asconar is renowned for her gentleness, her compassion, and her love of beauty; but she is no simpering noble's daughter raised only to the needle and the mirror. She is the third child of Eshut, Warrior Queen of Endor, and she met Alwick on a battlefield. They fought side by side in the Skirmish wars, and she took up her sword a second time when the Witch Queen stirred her armies in our more recent border conflict. Beneath her skill and her satin exterior is a warrior cut from steel, and she and I have more in common than many might think.

"I suppose you know about my forthcoming trip?" Alwick demanded of me, and I nodded.

"I do, Your Majesty. Master Lythian thought I should know, so that I could counter any rumour that might come to me."

"Hmm." Alwick glanced at his wife, who hid a smile behind her hand. "Lythian would, of course. The only ones supposed to know are the ones who are going. Which should leave you out." He considered me challengingly as he said this, but I decided not to rise to the implied bait.

"As my King desires," I acquiesced instead.

He snorted with amusement. "Bloodit, Parisan – I can't risk taking you, and you know it. I need to talk to Octian, and I won't be able to if you part his head from his shoulders – and you would, given half a chance, so don't deny it."

I didn't intend to. "My opinions concerning Carthery are public knowledge, Your Majesty," I said quietly. "But I would do nothing to imperil Your Majesty's diplomacy, unless I had no alternative."

Sharasaan chuckled softly. "Your Lady does not always offer you one," she pointed out. "And you would make the Duke nervous."

"She makes half my court nervous," Alwick added,

swigging at the contents of his goblet. "That's one of the reasons she serves me so well."

Foo panted a silent grin in agreement to that, his tail quivering with suppressed laughter. It is his habit to keep close-mouthed while in Alwick's presence, a gesture of respect that few can claim to have earned. While human lives are played out but the once, to Foo the aspect of kingship is one that belongs only to a mature soul. Since Alwick has long since proved his ability and worthiness to wear Asconar's crown, my R'rruthren Firstborn honours him with the deference due to a Hunter in his ninth life. Sharasaan winked at him, reaching down to pet one of the lion cubs who had now settled at her feet. I kept my face dispassionate, as always, and the King nodded a wry approval of my non-reaction. "The point is," he went on to say with a sigh, "that you were not invited. The Archmagus Reinwald was."

"The Archmagus? But surely the Lord Augis and Lady Deshart ..."

"Augis would make Octian as nervous as you would," Alwick butted in bluntly. "He's Oscallon trained and a specialist in glamour. I'm trying to give the appearance of honesty to this gathering."

"I understood the Duke to be no small master of magic himself," I pointed out, a little coldly, since I have heard rumours that do not speak well of the man's casting.

"He is an accomplished sorcerer," Sharasaan said softly. "And I doubt he would see Augis as a threat, but there may be others in his party less knowledgeable on such matters. Reputation is often more important than truth when it comes to appearances."

Foo suppressed a snort at that one, flexing his foreclaws in the rug beneath him. Alwick shot him a shrewd glance, then smiled at his queen. "They both know that well enough," he remarked dryly. "Deshart will be there, but her skill is manipulative, not protective. Reinwald has a certain ability with the suppressing of others' power and I proposed to the Duke that we established a neutral area within which magic would not function to either of our advantages."

"He agreed to that?" I questioned in some surprise. I had not known that Reinwald had any power of control in that fashion, but it would be a useful skill in several situations, this not least of them. I recalled Deckle's comment about his master having ways to keep his enchanted pieces slumbering, and the seeming absence of magic in the mage's workshop. My respect for the Archmagus increased considerably.

"He did." Alwick's reply was brusque. "Lythian informed me that he laughed before he agreed. I gather some of his councillors were less than happy at the concept. They suspect treachery, of course."

"Of course," I said. "They wouldn't be in Carthery if it wasn't always on their minds."

Sharasaan chuckled. Alwick glared at her before turning back to me. "Fortunately, Reinwald's reputation is one of impartiality. And precision. I remember him scouring the field at Tabworth – his whirlwind took down a thousand of the Harren, and not a pennant stirred among our ranks. He was the obvious choice. So where in the Seven Hells is he?"

"None of them, Your Majesty." I was sure on that point. "At least – the last time I looked, his soul flame still burned. Do you think some plot was hatched to remove him from the playing board?"

"I don't know what to think," the King admitted with a sigh. "What with young Broderick breaking the man's mirror, and asking you to find him before I even knew he was missing ... Confound the boy! Too eager to do the right thing without considering the consequences."

"He's young," the Queen interjected. "He will learn."

"Of course he will." Alwick was not really annoyed with his youngest son, merely angry with the situation. "But in the meantime, Parisan here is fighting gargoyles in the street for no apparent reason or result. You took no harm from that, I trust?"

I allowed myself the barest smile. "None that My Lady could not heal, Your Majesty."

He harumphed, disconcerted, as many can be, by my casual acceptance of my goddess' power. I have no choice, for she guides me from within and to refute her is to deny myself. "Well," he said, "we thank her for that. This matter must be settled, Pas, and soon."

There are few, in this world, who know me well enough to address me with such intimacy. Fewer that I would allow to do so. Alwick had been my father's friend, and has known me from my childhood; on his lips the shortening of my name is an appeal to the woman he knows lies beneath my armour, a woman who is his friend rather than his servant and whom he can trust beyond the ties of duty and loyalty alone. That cold and windswept day, when I fought to his side and greeted him in My Lady's name, he had accepted my transformation with sorrow. The Skirmish Wars had taken many of his best, but he had not expected my father to be one of them. I had ridden from the ruins of Orandy to fight at his side, bearing my chosen burden along with my father's banner, and he had taken my oath on the battlefield – naming me knight, but regretting the need for it. We had parted once as carefree friends, he the liege who treated me like royalty, I the child not yet quite a woman. We met again as Warlord King and Holy Paladin, the time we might have had lost and sullied by event. Yet he has not forgotten, and neither have I. There is a space between us now that all his kingship cannot fill, but a bridge remains and sometimes he reaches across it so that we meet halfway.

One of Foo's ears swivelled back in my direction, a twitch of attention that belied his apparently relaxed crouch. "What would you have me do?" I asked quietly. The king sighed, placing the now empty goblet back on the table.

"I'm not sure," he admitted. "Pas – if it were not for Broderick asking for your aid, I would not have chosen to involve you in this. I know what you think of politics. You serve me and the truth in equal measure, not the Kingdom above all things. I would the rest of the world were more like you in that, but they are not, and I must plot and counterplot in accord with the way things are, not the way they should be. I must compromise, and negotiate, where you would put honour and justice above any other considerations."

"Which is why," Sharasaan interrupted with a warm smile, "you are king and she is not. Am I not right, my lady?"

I acknowledged the jest with a tilt of my head, responding to her warmth with the barest smile of my own. There are some who might think I would envy Sharasaan, who won Alwick's heart with her sword where I lost it with mine. They know neither her, nor I, to judge such a thing. We might be friends, and perhaps we are, although circumstances dictate we never discuss it. Her love for her husband, the joy she finds in her sons – they are part of what I forswore when I took up my holy blade, but I harbour no jealousies toward her because of it. Instead I hold her in quiet regard, knowing her steel and the fire that lies beneath her silken gentleness. The truth of it is that Alwick loves her, and for that I am glad indeed. He threw her a mock frown which slipped into a real one as he tried to recollect where his words were leading. She was right, of course – I serve two masters, and while one may command my service, the other dictates my life. In that I cannot change, nor would I wish to. Alwick chose me to serve as his Investigator, bearer of his personal seal and authorised to command in his name should I have need, but he picks the services he asks of me with care, knowing my strengths and my purposes.

"It may be that there is intrigue behind the Archmagus' disappearance," the King continued, having recalled the direction of his thoughts. "The Duke has enemies who would delight in disrupting our meeting together. But if that is it, then they have played a very subtle hand indeed. I must know if such plotting is afoot – and Reinwald must be found. One may lead to the other, of course, but even if that proves a false trail, I want you to find him.

Do you have any idea as to what may have happened?"

I shook my head slowly. "The picture is not clear, Your Majesty. I am sure someone in the Archmagus' household knows something, and the attack yesterday was no mere coincidence – of that much I am certain. But beyond that I am hunting in the dark."

Alwick nodded, looking down at Foo rather than at me. "That has never stopped you before," he pointed out quietly.

"No," I agreed. "But determination does not always lead to success. I can make you no promises, my king."

"I'm not asking for them. I know you will do your best. Both of you," he added. "Go speak to Scarll. He's in the west tower, watching someone who has contacts he should not. Tell him to find out what the man knows – and help him if he has need of it. If the man has no wish to speak, remind him that I am more generous in dealing with traitors than the Duke of Carthery will ever be. And Pas..." He leant forward to emphasis his final point. "Be careful. Anyone who can make Reinwald vanish into thin air is someone to be reckoned with."

Chapter Nine

"Baron Sheerwater," the indolent voice drawled, "has been dabbling in matters that do not concern him." The voice's owner shifted forward, bringing his profile into the light, and smiled sweetly at the two of us. "I take it Alwick thinks it time he stopped?"

Scarll Scarlettini – Prince Scarll of the House of Scarlet, to give him his full title – is not, at first glance, a man to be trusted in anything. His demeanour screams decadence, from the scented oil that curls his dark hair, through the extravagant cut of his silk and velvet clothing, down to the silver and gem encrusted cane which he sports as a fashion prop. His voice enhances the impression, a bored drawl of disinterest that carries hints of arrogance among its tones. Only fools rely on first impressions, of course. Scarll is no more the dissolute fop than am I.

He is the king's brother-in-law, youngest first line son of the merchant house whose miraculous dyes and fabrics have made them the second most powerful influence in Daberon for decades. Any first line son of a Daberon House is entitled to be called Prince, of course, but Scarll is the genuine article, his family's power and influence extending back generations. His oldest sister, the Princess Eleana, married Alwick soon after he succeeded to the throne, and theirs would have been a long and comfortable marriage had fate not cut the threads of her life in the birthing of the Crown Prince. Despite, or perhaps because of, their mutual loss, Asconar and the House of Scarlet maintained their diplomatic association, and Scarll became a familiar sight among the interweavings of the court, ostensibly serving the interests of his House, apparently serving his own interests, and actually serving Alwick with shrewd sensibilities. Like me, he carries the King's Seal, although I doubt he would ever use it except in grave circumstances. To all intents and purposes he is still a foreigner at court, Daberon by birth and nature, and he likes to maintain the image since it suits both his needs and his preferences.

"We went hawking in the park this morning," Scarll continued distantly, arranging the lace on his cuff with meticulous care. "Poor weather for such sport, I said, and he laughed at me. Went anyway. Met a man from down river – who looked quite odd in worn leather. Better suited to velvet, I would say. Black velvet, at that," he added, turning to offer Foo a sly smile. Foo panted a silent laugh and twitched his whiskers. He likes Scarll, although I disapprove of the prince's influence. They have been known to go drinking together in the most disreputable of places. If Alwick has a man best placed to serve his interests where the Velvet City is concerned, it is probably Scarll, although I would not dream of asking him if it is so.

"What did they talk about?" I asked instead, leaning my armoured weight against the edge of the window seat and sweeping my gaze around the vaulted hall with studied indifference. We were gathered in the lowest chamber of the west tower, one of the court's favoured places for morning kafir and gossip in the autumn. It looks out into the formal gardens but is well sheltered and warmed by a series of hearth fires that yawn within the supporting pillars like the mouths of sleeping dragons. It would be abandoned once winter set in, shunned for more intimate rooms and warmer gatherings, but in early spring and late autumn it draws the morning courtiers who have time on their hands and cradles them in the curves of the carved sandstone and the bold tapestry work that adorns the walls.

"This and that," Scarll considered, smiling at a young lady who was passing by with her maidservant in attendance. The lady simpered in his direction, then dropped a startled half curtsey as she realised who kept him company. The maidservant dipped even further, nearly dropping the covered basket she was carrying. I tilted my head in acknowledgement and the two of them hurried away, both glancing back with wide eyes. The prince laughed. "You scare away my butterflies," he scolded without heat. "Even without your blessed blade."

"You will have time enough for that later," I answered coldly. Foo's tail quivered and he bounded up onto the window seat, pretending to look out of the window while he regained his composure. I ignored him. "What of the Baron?"

"Sheerwater? He smokes Fevule. His contact brought him more of it in exchange for gossip. The gossip," he added with a yawn, "went no further than the edge of the park."

I frowned at him, not liking the implications of that remark, and he threw me a wicked grin. "The man is in the hands of the Wardens," he explained patiently. "He still had enough unstamped Fevule on him to warrant several months in city labouring. The Wardens," he went on, "did not believe his claim to be a man of influence. If his fellows in Carthery have any taste they will leave him to rot for a while."

"Did he serve the Duke?"

"No." Scarll was dismissive of the idea. "Octian picks men with more discretion than that. More intelligence, too. Hunsana, possibly. Or Count Morgarran. They have more to lose if the Desina tightens his hold on the river trade."

I was not interested in the internal wranglings of Carthery's council and said as much, trying to keep impatience from my voice. Scarll laughed softly, withdrawing a handkerchief from his belt and dabbing at his nose with it. "The Baron will be in the gardens shortly," he announced with a hint of smugness. "Perhaps we should go and meet him."

***

Scarll walked ahead of us, his scarlet cloak shimmering as he passed from shade to sun and back again along the colonnaded walkways. Feathers tumbled from the elaboration of his hat, which was bedecked with dagging and overlaid with embroidery. Maris, his ever-present manservant, sulked at his heels, a brooding presence picked, it was said, as much to offset the man's elegance as he was for his skill as a valet. Foo paced beside me, flexing the claws on his right hand and using them to comb through his whiskers. Like many of his people, my faithful R'rruthren prides himself on his neatness and appearance, and Scarll's casual brilliance always brings out the fastidious streak in his nature. It amuses me a little to see them compete: stripped of his finery, Scarll would be an anonymous individual, devoid of any particularly outstanding feature, and he knows it. Foo's elegance and sleekness is inherent, not cultivated.

We reached an open space where half a dozen paths met and crossed, a statue of King Canthaw posed in its centre. Scarll went to lean on the old king's shoulder, casually ordering Maris to polish his already gleaming boot. Foo leapt to the top of a nearby urn and from there to the top of the stone lintel that lay over the path we had emerged from, losing himself in the tumble of autumn leafed vines that encrusted it. I stepped sideways into the shadow of a weathered pillar, murmured a quiet prayer for anonymity, and waited.

I did not wait long. Baron Sheerwater, a florid-faced noble who wore russet browns over the glint of his mail, swaggered into view almost to the second that Scarll had predicted. He had two men in tow, common armsmen who wore his livery. The Baron is a minor noble at court, one who had not had occasion to be brought to my attention before. I may have been prejudiced by Scarll's accounting of him, but I was not particularly impressed. He was tending towards portly, and his clothing showed signs of self-neglect. Normally this would have been merely an indication of slovenliness, but in his case it was undoubtedly a result of his private addictions. Fevule is a mild narcotic compared to some I could think of, but it dulls the mind while heightening appetites. It is not, strictly speaking, illegal, but it is heavily taxed, and its use is frowned upon by all but those with the most jaded of palettes. The taxes make it an expensive luxury, and those who succumb to it often slide into more esoteric abuses. Sheerwater might not have gone that far yet, but the signs of his decline were obvious if you knew where to look.

"Well met again, my lord baron." Scarlettini's greeting was bored and unsurprised. "Did you recover your bird?"

"I did," Sheerwater growled, "no thanks to you. You owe me a hundred crowns, my lord." The resentment he put into the honorific was laden with scorn. Scarll straightened slightly, his gem-topped cane dangling lightly from one hand.

"I owe nothing to traitors, Medrian Sheerwater. The bet was forfeit the moment you stopped to collect from your paymaster. You should have stayed with Sparkweed. The price it carries is not so high."

The Baron's eyes flared with anger and his hand dropped to his sword. "Do you accuse me of treachery?" he hissed.

The Merchant Prince smiled warmly. "Exactly," he said, with a hint of delight. "You are with us today, aren't you? The game is over, Baron." He lifted a finger to wag it scoldingly at the incensed noble. "Time to settle up. Pay the piper. The king requires a different tune from now on."

Sheerwater glanced around, then glowered at his accuser, the sword sliding easily from its sheath. "One word against another is not enough," he growled. "Can you prove your accusations?"

"No need," Scarll considered lightly, stepping back so that the statue gave him a little shelter from direct attack. Maris straightened up and stared at the nervous armsmen, who had not yet drawn their weapons. "Alwick knows all about your little weaknesses – and who feeds them. You owe him an explanation. I am merely here to collect the debt."

"Dead men collect nothing," Sheerwater spat.

"Especially dead popinjays." He motioned to his men, who drew sword and stood ready behind him. "I was planning to leave soon, anyway. I'll accept your prattling throat in exchange for my hundred crowns." He lunged forward, his blade striking sparks from the old king as Scarll slid under the statue's arm. Maris let out a rumbled growl and reached for the nearest armsman, who had barely time to lift his blade before he was engulfed in a determined bearhug. The second darted after his master, flanking the statue in order to strike from the other side, only to go down as a furred missile sprung at his face from above.

Only a fool faces a R'rruthren in such an attack. Foo leapt out with all claws extended, his lips drawn back in silent snarl, his weight aimed at the man's shoulders. He struck to subdue and capture, not kill – since he could have served that purpose well enough with a knife dispatched from his perch – but the man did not know that. All he saw was the savage gleam of teeth and wild eyes as his ambusher sprang over the length of his blade. The sword clattered to the gravel and the man followed, tumbled backwards by hissing and spitting weight, a cry of sheer terror escaping him. Sheerwater hesitated in his second lunge, distracted by the unexpected intervention in his attack. Scarll took the opportunity to dance back in my direction, knocking the Baron's sword aside with the reach of his cane. His attacker cursed and strode after him, pulling to a halt as I stepped out of the shadows.

"Baron Sheerwater," I pronounced coldly, Dancer's brightness gleaming between us. "You are a traitor to your king and a cowardly betrayer of your knightly vows. Three swords against two unarmed men? I do not call that justified combat."

Sheerwater hissed with surprise, anger still directing his actions. "This is not your quarrel, noble lady. Leave men's work to men and go play your games of knightly honour elsewhere."

"I play no games," I said tightly, " As you would do well to remember. But perhaps the smoke in your brain clouds your recollections. You may be in the pay of Carthery or you may not, but an attempt to murder the king's brother by marriage is treachery in anyone's book. Whatever he may have accused you of."

"I will silence his peacock tongue for once and for all," the baron roared, striking past me at Scarll's amused grin. His intended victim stepped back, and I deflected the blow with ease.

"Surrender to me," I suggested. "And Alwick will judge you fairly. His justice is more certain than Duke Octian's, should he hear of how you have conspired with his enemies." Sheerwater blanched a little at that, confirming our suspicions in a single reaction. Not the Duke's man, then, but one tempted by those who opposed him in subtle ways.

"Never," he decided. "I will never surrender to a woman and a fop."

"Then yield to your knightly better," I said, unmoved by his intended insult. His answer was a curse and a lunge of his blade. Dancer's edge sparked as she took the force of the blow.

We fought there, gravel shifting beneath our feet, blade ringing crisply against blade in the autumn air. He outreached me by several inches; I outmatched him by several more. His style was predictable; he used no fancy work but straightforward blows designed to wear down and overwhelm an opponent by strength and determination. He would have fought well in the Border conflicts, cutting through swathes of Harren rabble with brutal sweeps of his blade. My art is more directed, more precise. I met blow with deflecting angle, sweep with yielding step, each strike seemingly his, each piece of strength he paid my victory. I could have had him early; he exposed his weaknesses without being aware of them, but I wanted him alive – and unharmed if I could manage it. It is not often that I practice my swordplay against a determined opponent, and his arrogance was in need of deflation. I played with him, Dancer answering to my hand with easy certainty.

I had fought the day before, steel ringing against unyielding stone, Kirby's easy comradeship at my shoulder. This was no comparison to that. There had been an urgency, a desperate danger, in that conflict, and with it the warm strength of My Lady, arming me for battle. This time I fought alone, sustained only by my own skill and energies. I had laughed then, lifted by the gift that made me what I am; I did not laugh now, only fought with icy certainty and cold contempt. He began with anger. It gave way to alarm and desperation.

We danced, my blade and I, weaving steel before his eyes in patterns of autumn sunlight. He struck again and again at the shimmer it raised, never finding an opening, never reaching beyond my studied defence. I drove him back to seek shelter behind the coldness of stone. Once again, Dancer's blade struck sparks from carved arms, but these had no power to move and fell easily to my blows.

Someone was laughing and cheering my work; I ignored the distraction and focused my deliberation down to a single aim. Sheerwater's anxiety became fear. His attack became a defence that staggered before the pattern of my blade. Sweat beaded his brow and blurred his eyes. Dancer flew and parried with surgical precision, driving back his blows with easy victory.

"Sorcery," he gasped as I backed him into a pillar where he was forced to stand.

"Skill." I refuted his words with cold tones. "Dancer's enchantment is to serve and never break. I have no need of magic to defeat your ilk, Sheerwater." I drove forward and twisted, shearing his sword close to the hilt. He glanced down at the broken edge, then gave an incoherent cry and turned to flee.

Foo was waiting for him with a drawn knife and a dagger-toothed grin.

"Bravo," Scarll applauded, emerging back into the open. He glanced at Maris and waved an idle hand in his direction. "Find us a couple of Ravens," he commanded. The hulking figure nodded and left; the sound of sword play is not unknown in the palace gardens and it would take more than that to attract even the most vigilant of guards. I glanced round as he left, wondering what had become of the Baron's armsmen while we fought, and found them crumpled in a snoring heap next to a vine wrapped pillar. Both fast asleep, it seemed. I frowned and glanced at Foo, whose nose and whiskers were twitching a little – but with pent up energy rather than an impending sneeze. One of Scarll's tricks then – perhaps a pinch of enchanted dust, or something equally subtle.

"Well, Sheerwater," the Prince's lightly accented voice was drawling. "Ready with that explanation now?"

The Baron cursed, backing away from Foo's challenging stare. The tips of my friend's ears barely reached a point level with the man's chest, but his four and half feet of muscle and fur armed with teeth, claws and gleaming blade can be an extremely intimidating sight. "I beg the king's mercy," Sheerwater panted, turning towards me in appeal. I slid Dancer back into her scabbard and considered him coldly.

"You may get it," I allowed. "If we hear the truth from you. What word did you pass to your paymasters, and what more did they desire?"

He stared at me, reaching to wipe the sweat from his forehead. He was panting for breath, his face lined with exhaustion. I was barely breathing hard. "It was nothing, I swear. Word of the gathering of the Lions, and the names of those due to serve the King in the Dosefar roster."

I glanced at Scarll, who looked sceptical. "The Lions are all above suspicion," he decided wearily. "But I can look into that. What else, Sweatwater?"

The baron shook, haggard realisation replacing his earlier arrogance. "The comings and goings of Prince Rufus, and who is in favour with him," he said, wincing a little at the frown this wrote on the Daberon's face. Scarll is very fond of his nephew and would be most upset if anything ever happened to him. One elegant hand twisted on the top of the cane, revealing the snick of steel and an inch of shining blade concealed within its length before he recovered enough to resecure its hiding place. I should have known Scarll would have some means of defending himself.

"And...?" he prompted, dispelling the frown with a bored yawn. Foo added to the prompt by ostentatiously tossing the dagger from one hand to the other and echoing the yawn, but without the polite covering gesture of hand and lace trimmed wrist. Sheerwater went an interesting shade of grey.

"That is all, I swear it. I am paid to let certain shipments pass though my lands without question, no more than that. The words were extra favours, nothing more. I meant no treachery."

"Just the feeding of a jaded appetite," I observed cuttingly. "Is a moment's pleasure worth more to you than your king, or your people? What else were you promised? Money? Power? Other pleasures? Or perhaps revenge motivates your dealings. Has the king offended you? The Archmagus slighted you at court?"

It was a wild guess, and it brooked no reaction other than puzzlement. "I honour the king," he protested, although a little unconvincingly.

"By stabbing him in the back?" Scarll said wryly. "Very honourable, I'm sure. Ah, my Ravens."

Maris reappeared, four grim faced Ravens in tow. Scarll advised them that the matter was in the King's hands and they gathered up the unconscious armsmen and carted off the Baron, who went with reluctance. Scarll waved daintily as the man disappeared through the pillared ways, and then turned to me with a sigh.

"Cold trails," Foo observed, sheathing his knives and his claws together. "Old spoor. If this tangled corruption has anything to do with our hunting he didn't know about it."

"I'm sorry, my lady," Scarll apologised. "All that exercise for little return. I doubt me the Baron's paymasters know much about the King's business, except that something is afoot. Rufus is our smokescreen," he explained as I frowned at this conclusion. "He's the one due to go drake hunting in the marsh edges at Towerstele."

Foo grinned. "The perfect place to meet a ruler of swamp and waterways," he laughed. "A pretty thought, friend Scarlettini. Duke Octian sneaking down the river to conspire in the mud of his borders."

"Hush," I commanded, not unkindly. Hawksley Lodge is based on the coast north of the Medlure's delta and the city it supported. Towerstele is on the river itself, some hundred miles south and west of the true meeting place. If Rufus chose to go hunting at the edge of Carthery's domain that was his affair, but it would offer the perfect opportunity to obscure his father's purposes. Scarll was right – the conspirator's interest in the prince pointed to them being unaware of the details of the proposed meeting they intended to disrupt. It was doubtful they had had anything to do with Reinwald's disappearance, since he was part of the detail they were trying to identify.

"I doubt," Scarll observed, a little fastidiously, "that Octian Desina would think much of mud, whether it was his or not." He pronounced the Duke's family name with the Dethick emphasis that turned its central 'i' into an elongated 'e', earning himself a tilted ear twitch from Foo and a grunt from Maris. I let my lips curl into the hint of a smile.

"Perhaps not," I acknowledged softly. "They do say there is Daberon blood in the old Carthery lines, don't they?"

He bristled almost visibly, then burst out laughing. "Oh, my lady," he chuckled, "I deserved that, did I not? As ready with your wit as with your sword – and I defenceless on either hand when facing your beauty. I bow to your blow with honour." And he did so, a low sweep of elegance that involved a doffing of his hat and a quivering of white and scarlet lace. Foo swiped a casual hand at the temptation of his feathers, which Scarll fended off good naturedly. "I must away," he decided.

"The King will wish my news from this morning's work, and I am keeping you from yours. Good hunting!"

Foo answered him with a snarling yowl, the tongue twisting R'rruthren response to the familiar parting wish. I merely saluted him – open heart, open hand; the customary gesture of a knight to an equal. I am King's Investigator, he King's Conspirator, but we are comrades and I have a sneaking fondness for the man. He, like me, is never quite what he seems.

***

"So now where do we seek our trail?" Foo asked as we made our way to the outer gates of the palace.

"Where we left it," I answered promptly. "With two dead thieves and a suspect household. I think all this talk of politics has befuddled matters as much as sweetsmoke has befuddled Sheerwater's mind. Kirby is right – most of the traffic that comes up river is tainted with Black Velvet one way or another, and we should not confuse diplomatic paranoia with simple greed. On the whole, very few people are driven by ideals and higher motives."

"You are," he pointed out, matching his easy lope to my pace with long habit. The look he got back held affectionate exasperation.

"I have no choice in the matter."

He laughed. "I know," he said. "Else you would have spitted the Baron the first chance you had, not played him like a fish on a long line. Cruel, you are, just like a woman of my people, teasing helpless prey."

I suppressed a grin, knowing that to be a compliment. R'rruthren do not hunt for sport alone, but they do take pleasure in the process. "He needed a lesson. He'd have spitted Scarll had I not been there to stop it."

"Not the Scarlet prince, sweet lady. He's got more lives than I have."

That was irresistible. I laughed, despite myself, and the Ravens on the gate must have wondered at the unexpected sight. Foo grinned and bounded ahead, leading the way along the ancient King's Road toward the waiting slopes of Raven's Hill. I shook my head at his enthusiasm and followed with a measured pace, turning my thoughts to the mystery we still pursued and the manner in which our hunt might yet regain its elusive trail.

***

"... and so I have reason to believe that the night before last was not the first time that the thief came to this house. I want you all to think back and try to recall if you have seen anyone resembling either of these two men in the past."

I was standing in the main room of Reinwald's house, the members of his household gathered round me, while Foo watched alertly from the doorway. I had explained some of the events of the previous day, avoiding too direct an accusation and leaving out the fate of Usurus. The reactions of my suspects were interesting, if not particularly enlightening.

Mac Doonin clearly thought my words held no importance for him; he kept his face carefully neutral, while his eyes betrayed a hint of disdain. He had struck me as having a slightly selfish edge, a young man with too much confidence in himself and his abilities. He had expressed concern about his master, and his greeting had demanded further news, but my tale of two thieves and their falling out appeared to spark nothing more than disinterest. I wondered whether the length of his study under Reinwald would have given him the strength to bring stone to life. This was not a house of Elementalism, but the Archmagus appeared to have encompassed many skills and it might be that he had taught his apprentices to take a similar approach to their use of power.

Deckle fidgeted. My arrival had dragged him away from some experiment or other, his appearance in the main room being followed by a trail of blue and green smoke. His questions concerning my success had been intense and anxious, betraying either his real concern for Reinwald, or else a fear that I might have uncovered his part in the Mage's disappearance. He listened to me with distracted attention, his mind clearly not on the tale at all.

Young Hal Markstele, on the other hand, was wide eyed and totally fascinated. I doubted very much that he had any hand in the business, but it is not impossible to encounter an old head on young shoulders and I could not eliminate him entirely. He seemed greatly taken by the description of the finding spell, and tugged at Mac Doonin's robe to ask if he might learn such a thing. Mac Doonin's answering nod held a hint of impatience, but the assent was not begrudged.

The housekeeper was too busy being outraged to convey any other emotion. She'd not been at all happy to welcome us, probably associating our arrival with yet more disaster to come. She interrupted me more than once, questioning whether my tale was suitable for young ears, and passing comments about 'those' that lived in Gutterside. If it was an act, it was a good one; if not I had given her plenty of material for indignant marketplace gossip for weeks to come.

Eachan simply glared at me. Not openly; he was far too conscious of his place in the household to appear directly contemptuous, but his eyes held smouldering resentment from the minute he saw us arrive. He fiddled with a ring that he wore on his crippled hand as I talked, pretending not to pay attention. I caught a brief glimpse of a sneer on his lips as I spoke of the Wardens, and I wondered if he had sought employment there and been rejected because of his injury.

I waited at the end of my speech, but no-one claimed any knowledge of the thief or his partner. Theda was of the opinion that any such low life would have been seen off the premises with ill favour, which managed to produce a genuine smile on the handyman's otherwise cynical face, and Mac Doonin simply said that his Master dealt with many sorts and he'd never stopped to ask if any of them stole for a living. Deckle hesitantly ventured that perhaps it had been Reinwald himself selling his craft, a thought that had not occurred to me, and was briefly tempting – except that the Archmagus would have found better outlets with far more discrete dealers than an opportune thief and his greedy partner. I made a mental note to check whether Reinwald had shown any evidence of trouble with his finances recently while the doubt filled apprentice stuttered an apology for making the suggestion in the first place. I had no doubt that Mac Doonin's angry glance had something to do with his change of mind.

I thanked them for their attention and promised I would return as soon as I had any further news. Foo muttered an opinion that the whole visit had been a waste of time, and I was half inclined to agree with him. Certainly I had failed to identify which of the mage's household might be concealing knowledge of his disappearance, and if our unknown suspect had a guilty conscience concerning their thievery no-one had shown any evidence of it. All the same I was left with the impression that I had somehow unravelled another inch of the Spinner's thread from the Weaver's Loom, even if I could not yet identify where it might start or end.

We were left alone in the entrance hall, Foo having paused to brush down my cloak before he handed it to me. I remembered that I had one more thing to check before we left and waved at him to stay put, turning to make my way up the stairs. Mac Doonin had already escorted his fellow apprentices onto the first floor and I saw no sign of any of them as I crossed the landing and ascended the second flight. On the second floor I turned my steps down the passageway towards the Archmagus's study and came to a halt before the doors. Above me Reinwald's soul flame still shone, flickering fitfully in the shadowed corridor. The Magus still lived, wherever he might be, a fact which reassured me a little as I stood in the hallway and watched the pattern of light inside the crystal globe. It was not as bright as it had been the day before, and I realised that the time I had to find the missing man was limited.

Had I the Summoner's art, or even a hint of the power Reinwald was supposed to hold, I might have had a chance to locate him through that intricate piece of crafting. Such a working is beyond me, and I knew of no-one in the city upon whom I could prevail for such a task. There are those, the infamous Thurston Rawnsley among them, whom I might call upon in other circumstances, but they do not dwell in Asconar, and would need greater reason than the fate of one man to make use of their power.

I left the flicker of light and returned to the hallway, where I found Foo chatting to the timid maid I had interviewed before. She was giggling at some remark or other and I halted on the stairway so as not to disturb them. There are many among the everyday folk of our world who find me intimidating, and I have found Foo's easy manner and deceptive charm will often encourage confidence where my own presence inspires awed silence. It is the same disarming manner that allows many a R'rruthren to negotiate favourable prices or extract themselves from awkward situations. Of course, the listener must be open to such charm; the angry mob from whose hands I had once liberated my faithful companion had been in no mood for words, measured or otherwise. It had not been easy to counter their accusations, and the proof that had lifted their blood price from his head had not been cheaply bought. The price had been a worthy one, however – it had brought me his friendship and if any debt is owed between us now it must surely be in my hands to redeem, not his.

I waited until the exchange of words seemed complete before I chose to disturb the two of them. I strode down the remaining steps with regal authority and the maid practically took to her heels. Foo watched her go, his whiskers twitching with a hint of laughter. He turned to me with a white toothed grin, his ears forward and his eyes sparkling. "That was a cruel entrance," he purred, lifting my cloak and standing on tiptoe so he could reach to drape it around my shoulders. "You frighten her as much as her Master does."

I smiled wryly, fastening the clasp at my throat and directing him towards the door. "'Those who do not choose to look will never see'," I quoted. "I was not called for the frightening of maidservants, any more than you are called to flatter them. Did she have words for us?"

He nodded and opened the door for me, waiting until we were out in the courtyard before he spoke. "Our friend Kerkle came to the house several times," he said softly. "He had beguiling words for a bored drudge and earned himself a stolen slice of cake or two in the process. She did not know who he came to see, but they met in the stable-house, late in the evening mostly. He promised her trinkets for her silence, and she kept it. She thought him a handsome rogue, but feared him, all the same."

"The young lady fears many things," I remarked, drawing my hood up against the squally weather. "But her story confirms what we thought. She had no idea whom he came to see?"

"None," he sighed. "She has little curiosity, and less ambition, that one."

"Probably why Theda employed her." I echoed his sigh, leading our way down the hill. "This labyrinth is a collection of solid walls and few passages. We have need of better directions if we are to find our way out of it."

"For sure," he agreed. "But how do we find them?"

"By retracing our steps a little," I announced, lengthening my pace with determination. "And paying heed to the fragment of map we have already seen."

Chapter Ten

"I have nothing more to say to you," Linnell insisted with a hint of resentment. We were sat in Kirby's office where Bardoff had brought her at my request. Kirby himself was absent, dealing with a minor matter somewhere else in his district, but I had no fear he would object to my questioning the woman. She was not even his prisoner; she'd been offered the protection of the Ward House and had taken it with grateful relief. Being Kerkle's woman would have given her a status that his death would have erased. Without him she might be forced to return to the doubtful profession from which he had rescued her, and the respite that the Wardens provided (however brief it might prove to be) must have been a welcome one. Her original confusion had been replaced with sullen acceptance. She expected nothing from anybody and was certainly not about to offer anything to me simply out of the goodness of her heart. I heard Foo breath a quiet sigh; he clearly considered our conversation to be a waste of time.

"You know that Usurus is dead?" I asked, trying to judge whether her reticence was deliberate or simply due to mistrust.

"I know," she answered. "I know how he died, too." Her face held a hint of wary terror that she fought hard to keep under control. "That stone was accursed, wasn't it?" she decided suddenly, glaring at me as if I might somehow be responsible. "Curse the damned day he ever laid eyes on it. I wish I'd never looked into its star filled heart!" She choked back a sob of distress and wiped angrily at the corner of her eye with her sleeve.

"All things precious attract the curse of greed," I told her softly. "But that does not make them accursed of themselves. You need have no fear of harm befalling you."

135

"No harm?" Her laugh was bitter and accusatory. "My man belly up in a pool of his own blood, and the black heart that killed him torn to shreds in the street? The room was rented in his name. I have no home, no place to go, no one to protect me, and you say no harm will come? Lady, you have an honest heart, but such things are rare in my world. I'm bound for the gutter and you know it; that or the mattress turning, for reeking slobs to paw at as they please. Spare me your preaching, it has no hope of helping me."

I bent my head at the rebuke. She was right, of course. Her life had already been ruined by events, although I suspected that half Linnell's problems stemmed from her own poor opinion of herself. "Where would you wish to go had you the chance?" I asked, half from curiosity, half from calculation.

"There's none for me," she growled. "Chances are for the blessed, not the cursed. I was born in the Gutter and I'll probably die in it too. Literally, I should think."

Foo smothered a wry snort at this and I threw him a warning look. "No doubt you will," I observed, "if you have no other expectations. But there are always chances if you look hard enough." I reached into my breastplate and drew out the purse that nestled there. It was well weighted, since I can never be certain as to when I might need the magic that gold alone can wreak. Linnell's eyes widened at the gesture. "It is a pity," I went on thoughtfully, "that you have nothing more to tell me. Information can have value in many places – if offered to the right people."

"Well now," she said hurriedly. "It may be there's a word I could find, if I had an idea of where to start it."

"No," I shook my head, while Foo's tail quivered with silent laughter at my dissemblance. "You've chosen your path, Linnell. I am not one to turn you in other directions." I started to hang the purse at my belt and made as if to rise. She grabbed at my arm to restrain me, then drew back her grip in wary alarm.

"I might be thinking of the country," she gabbled, then

threw her head into her hands. "Must I beg?" she sobbed. "I will not ask for charity, my lady. I have my pride."

I took pity on her distress and sat back into the carved shape of my chair. "Do not call it charity," I said sternly. "My Lady's words are strict on that. Help to the helpless, strength to the weak, aid to those in distress; all are offered by her children, without conditions, but with clear judgement. Everything has its price, and nothing comes for free. Her Son pays for the world's suffering and we who serve her know that when we reduce that, we reduce his pain also. Charity is a gesture made without thought, directed without intent. I do not offer you that. Merely a chance to be more than you are. But I must be sure you will benefit from such a gifting – otherwise I will spend my coin on better deeds."

She stared at me, wrestling with a concept she had never been taught to even consider, let alone understand. My faith and my creed are not an easy path to follow. "I have to earn it? Is that how you're saying it? And watch what I'd do with it, after? I'd not spend it on drink, if that's your fear. I've a cousin, up on the coast. I could go to her. I've never seen the sea."

I let my eyes soften a little. "It's a sight that is hard to forget." I had not meant to distress her. She had information I needed, and needed badly, and I had thought to bargain for it as if I sought it in an alehouse. Recent events had hollowed out the strength with which she had been able to survive the streets; her bitterness was born of genuine despair, not hardened cynicism.

She considered me for a moment longer, then turned her head away. "It's of no account," she decided softly. "I cannot earn anything from you. I have nothing to say."

"Are you certain?"

She sighed heavily. "Kerkle is dead. Swelm is dead. What more is there in the tale? All else I know is gossip, which would have no use to such as you. Leave me to the Gutter, my lady. Take your coin and spend it on another lost soul. What could I do to warrant such saving?"

I glanced at Foo before I spoke. His upper lip was curled with wry patience, his eyes half closed, and the end of his tail twitched slightly as he watched us both. He had no expectations of this interview and was trying to be bored without being impolite.

"You could tell me about the Magpie," I said softly, bringing Linnell's head up in wide-eyed surprise, and Foo's ears bolt upright from their slow droop. I did not need to see the sudden narrowing of his eyes or the crease of puzzlement that wrinkled his brow to know that he would work out my reasoning; I was watching the woman as she struggled with her confusion, only to replace it with a wry smile of hope.

"He was right, weren't he?" she marvelled, looking at me with renewed respect. "About you knowing many things. Of course he'd have gone to him – he'd not ask questions. I'd just… never put mind to it before."

"So, tell me," I said, patting at the purse without making the gesture too obvious. I would have given her the money anyway, but she was not to know that – and would feel better about taking it if she thought it well earned. Her face narrowed down into a wary frown.

"I don't know much," she admitted. "Gossip, as I said before. Words on the street, and tales – you know." I nodded, while Foo leant forward, his ears twisting to catch her words as her voice dropped into conspiratorial tones. "There's a man, they say, and a place to take things – odd things, shiny things, things that might have value but no worth of coin on the street. He pays for some, sells others, without question. He knows, they say, about curses and," her voice went even quieter as she half mouthed the next word, "magic. But he's no book man. No spell caster. Just someone who knows."

"And how does anyone find him?"

Her face fell. "I don't know. Not in the Gutter, I know that much. Across the river I've heard, but I don't know where."

Across the river … My mind went back to the path we had pursued the previous day, the path of Swelm Usurus once he had left his partner dead in Packer's Street. Somewhere between that moment and the time of his death he had exchanged the Star Diamond for coin; somewhere on that twisted route between Waterdock and the Inner City.

"We will find him," I assured Linnell. She still looked doubtful, as if suspecting that her words had not been worth much.

"They say he's well protected," she hazarded. "That he has powerful friends …"

"I bet," Foo growled softly. She jumped and glanced at him in alarm, as if she had forgotten he was there.

My hand went to the crystal at my throat and I smiled coldly."Perhaps I will be one of them."

***

"How did you know?" Foo asked me as we made our way down to Fisher's Drop and the waiting river.

I shrugged. "I didn't. I guessed."

He threw me a sceptical look. "Nobody *guesses* a thing like that. Had you heard of this man somewhere before? I've heard him mentioned, the once, but not in a way to place him with this business. Who gave you the name?"

"Usurus," I answered promptly, attracting the attention of a bored boatman with a wave of my hand.

"Usurus?" He looked a little startled. "You never spoke to him." He eyed the approaching boat with distrust, and the boatman eyed him back with equal wariness.

"No, but Hyatt did, remember?"

He dropped into the craft with a light leap and reached back a hand to help me down, steadying the vessel with an easy balance. "But Hyatt said he made no sense in his dying words. Just cursed a lot."

I sat on the passenger bench, pausing to direct our ferryman across the river before formulating my reply. "Hyatt said a great deal more than that. He said Usurus bragged that 'he' would not find it now, and then spoke of a Linnet and a Magpie. He wasn't raving. He was trying to tell us something. For Linnet I read Linnell – the name is lifted from that of the bird – and all I had to do …"

"… was ask about the Magpie!" Foo laughed, a low rumble that made the boatman row a little faster. "You make the reasoning of your mind sound so simple, and yet you snatch onto the slightest thing that would pass another by without comment."

"I too am a hunter," I reminded him, and his ears flicked back as he chuckled at the thought.

"Faint trails and concealed spoor," he muttered. "It would help if we knew what we were hunting."

"True," I sighed. I paid the boatman a quarter crown and he tugged his hat in respect as we scrambled up the steps onto the quay. Waterdock was just as busy as it had been the day before, men loading and unloading the low decked river traders that jostled for space along the river bank. Autumn is a time for hurried trade, merchants eager to move their goods before winter slows their pace and prevents passage on many routes. Half the warehouses in Waterdock carry Daberon house markings, since there are few places indeed where the Merchant princes do not have a major hand upon the trade routes. I wondered if this man we sought, the Magpie, might be housed in such a place. A Daberon has less of an eye for the law than he does for a profit – no doubt there were many things that passed by under the eyes of both the Wardens and the King's custom men, disguised as innocent goods. Daberon shares a border with Asconar, but its trade routes entangle the whole of the Known Kingdoms in a common web. It would be easy enough to move contraband goods through the Hoomin Downs and along the borders of Kharad lands before bringing them into Asconar.

Of course, the Medlure rises close to the Daberon border, flowing across the southern end of Asconar before emptying into the sea right where Carthery spreads its tangled nets. If the houses of the Merchant Princes are first among the trade upon the land, then the ships of the Desinas carry that flag to sea. Duke Octian's influence extends far beyond his Velvet City because of it – no doubt one of the reasons Alwick had chosen diplomacy over hostility when it came to dealing with him. For all the much-vaunted independence of the Known Kingdoms, their major cities are woven together by subtle threads that cannot be seen but are felt almost every day.

We had passed a great many warehouses the previous day, and I was not about to search each and every one of them. I had a better idea of where to pursue the location of my quarry and I led my companion down past the hustle of the main Tradeway and into a side street off Tunners Lane. There is an ale-house I know, tucked away from the bustle of the warehouses and frequented by local men rather than passing boatmen or other strangers to the city. It is a well-established place that does not advertise its presence over much, relying on word of mouth to spread its reputation. There are many such establishments within the city walls, some of which are better known than others, but this particular one caters for the less business-minded of Waterdock's inhabitants and is a good place to purchase information – or other things, if you know how.

Foo adopted a laughing grin as he came to realise our intended destination. My faithful assistant is no stranger to the alehouses and taverns of Nemithia, although he is no great indulger in spirits or other intoxicants. It is curiosity that takes him into many places, and I have had reason to be grateful for it on more than one occasion. Often, while I must stand with dutiful attendance in the formal swirl of the court, he can be found dicing with knuckle bones in the most insalubrious of drinking dens, or perhaps conversing with trail-weary mercenaries and adventurers over a pint of ale. I never ask where he goes on such occasions, but he often returns with information that proves invaluable – if not to myself, then to others of the king's hands who serve Alwick in many ways.

The Bolt and Pallet was relatively empty at this time of the day. It was early yet, not quite the twelfth watch, and most of its usual clientele were probably either working, or not yet woken. I drew my cloak closely around me as I descended the steps into the bar's dim interior, the shimmer of its silver bells effectively cloaking the murmur of my armour as I walked. My head was bare for once, my helm still under the care of Garrick's skilled hands, and I murmured soft words that added a layer of obscurement to my appearance. Few even looked up as we entered, those that did more drawn to the agile form of my companion than to me. Foo bounded ahead to claim a discrete table in a shadowed alcove, and I followed him, drawing the attention of the barman as I passed.

The figure in the leather apron waved an acknowledgement, indicating he would be with us shortly, and I slipped into the seat Foo indicated – actually a cut-down barrel, stuffed and padded – and took a thoughtful look around. The Bolt is a working man's establishment, designed simply for drink and talk without any extra frills. The tables are simple slabs of wood balanced on old barrels, and the seats are equally rough cut and polished. There are private rooms for hire above the main taproom where personal business may be conducted, but it is not the sort of place to find merchants in conversation with others of their kind. Its most usual clientele are loaders and their ilk, along with the less salubrious of Waterdock's inhabitants.

There were two small groups of warehouse workers gathered at the tables, each sharing a jug of the house ale, and a scattering of other customers leaning on the bar or seated close to the fire. There was even the angular shape of a Phraif resting her abdomen on a stool and her lower elbows on a table so she could dip her tubular tongue into a filled goblet. Her multi-faceted eyes turned in my direction as I identified her presence. She was painted with the colours of the manual class and wore the Phairfaneffra Hive banding across her thorax. A simple worker, probably tasked with a collection or delivery. Her kind were a common sight in some parts of the city, and this one seemed perfectly at home in the Bolt. The workmen had eyed Foo with some surprise, but no-one made any comment. After a moment or two the brawny-armed barman made his way to our table and looked at me with vague hostility.

"This bain't be the place for no lady," he growled at Foo warily. My companion panted a quiet laugh, presumably resisting the temptation to growl back.

"Tell *her* that," he advised, curling his tail around the tuck of his feet on the barrel seat. The barman turned to me, opening his mouth to repeat the statement. I cut him short by tossing a half-crown onto the table in front of me.

"Chryskaan," I ordered, in a tone that brooked no argument. "Two cups and make them clean ones."

"Aye," he nodded, hesitating before he snatched up the coin and tested it with his thumbnail. I don't pass false coin, but silver is undoubtedly a rare sight in the Bolt's coffers. "Anything else?"

I looked up at him, feigning a bored expression. "Tell Magrath I'd like to see him," I said, as if I didn't really care one way or the other. His face darkened considerably.

"Master Magrath is busy," he announced. "He don't see no-one without no appointment."

Foo stretched up a little, flexing the claws on one hand idly into his shoulder fur. "Then make one," he suggested. "But don't keep the lady waiting."

The barman frowned thoughtfully before grunting and turning away. He brought back two plain goblets which he placed ungraciously in front of us, then vanished into the back room behind the dark curtain that divided it from the public room. Foo reached out and sniffed at the drink, his nose wrinkling up at the sharpness of the scent.

"Brew mellowed," he snarled softly, then took a deep swallow. "But fair of fire," he concluded, drawing air over his tongue with an appreciative hiss. I took a more cautious sip of the dark blue liquid, tasting the bitter herbs that had been dissolved into the spirit. Brew mellowed: good Chrsykaan is matured in scented wood barrels, the herbs regularly replaced over a period of years before it reaches a true fiery depth that cannot be imitated. This was cheap and the taste forced, but it had a good bite to it all the same.

The burly barman reappeared, looking across at us warily as he moved to serve one of the small groups of loaders. Shortly afterwards a dumpy figure in a dark jerkin emerged from behind the curtain and scowled in my direction. I brushed away the layer of obscurity I had placed around myself, and the scowl became a flutter of recognition. Doubtful relief settled on the man's face as he hurried over to our chosen corner, swiping a mug of ale out of a customer's hands as he passed.

"You honour me, my lady." He swept a chair across to our table and sank into it. I considered him without comment for a moment or two and he had to wipe away the perspiration that gathered on his forehead, taking a large gulp of the ale to cover his nervousness. Mugs Magrath – owner of the Bolt and Pallet, a man renowned both for his capacity for his own ale and as a notorious information broker – is afraid of me. He'd never admit it, of course, but it shines through every one of his perspiring pores whenever we come face to face. I think it may have something to do with my reputation, since Magrath has never seen me so much as raise a hand to anyone, but his skill in gathering and collating minor scraps of rumour and event can only have added to his opinion of me, not detracted from it. For all his fear, and Magrath is a man who fears many things for many reasons, he considers me one of the more welcome of his other kind of customer, and the smile he tentatively offered me was a genuine one.

"I need an address," I said, watching him struggle between his discomfort at my presence and his desire for the gold he knew I carried. He shrugged nervously.

"I woulda come if you'd sent word. There was no need

to lower yourself to my humble ale house. Honoured as I am," he added warily. I avoided the temptation to smile, maintaining my normal aloof expression.

"I was passing," I told him dryly. "From the taste of your Chryskaan, I should have kept going."

His face fell, and he shuffled his feet under the table. "I don't serve your kind of quality, my lady," he apologised. "Tha' knows that. My word is better than my spirits. But not so cheap," he added, glancing round in case we were being overheard. Foo leant back and let his mouth drop open a little. Magrath always amuses him, whether we meet in his own unsavoury surroundings or elsewhere in the city.

"That's because you have a healthy appetite to support," Foo remarked, licking the last of the liquor from his lips with a sweep of his tongue. Magrath threw him a look that might have intimidated anyone else. My friend merely twitched his whiskers a little.

"Ten crowns," I said, matching my words with the right number of coins placed between us. The information broker's eyes narrowed a little. That's a good month's wages for a loader or porter, and probably more than this particular information was worth, but I like to keep Magrath sweet for when I have need of more specialised knowledge. Foo hissed a little beside me, obviously thinking it was too much, or else not wanting the man to think I was foolishly generous in my dealings. After a moment the man's hand reached out so that he could cover the gleam of gold with his palm. He did not pull it towards himself – not yet – but his fingers twitched, and he looked back at me with calculating eyes.

"Just an address? Or an address and forgetting I've given it? Will it be a welcome visit to the man – or woman – that you seek?" Magrath was not seeking a moral judgement on his right to offer the information when he asked that particular question – merely attempting to add to his own knowledge. Now I did smile, a cold reminder that I was the one paying for information, not selling it. His curiosity subsided abruptly.

"I have not been here," I said softly. "Nor have you seen me. My business is not yours, Magrath. You would do well to remember that. Ten crowns – for the location of the Magpie."

He went a little white. "The Magpie? You know about the Magpie?"

"She knows many things," Foo growled, leaning forward. "Spit it up, or spit it back, Mugs. I wouldn't be so generous."

The man's hand curled more tightly over the gold. Magrath rarely fails me with coin to tempt his tongue. When he has no information he is usually honest enough to say so, unlike some of my sources. He may not be the most savoury of characters, but he is consistent – and, as I said, he is afraid of me. "Last I heard," he offered after a moment, "he might be found in the theatre business."

I waited. Mugs smiled hesitantly, glancing at Foo – who yawned indolently. A R'rruthren yawn is a spectacular sight at the best of times, all red tongue and teeth ending in a controlled clash. Magrath jumped as the daggered jaws snapped shut, looking back at me with a nervous twitch in his cheek. "The Paradoxican," he gulped, his eyes darting around in case he might be overheard. "That was the place. But the Magpie is a shy bird – it don't come out for a crowd. Nor an audience," he added, gabbling a little as he rushed to impart what he knew before anyone else might become interested. "You won't find him when there's a performance. Only at other times. Knock on the lowest door. He might let you in, but he doesn't always. Don't say I sent you."

"I won't," I assured him dryly. His eyes lingered on my face a moment longer, then he scooped the gold off the table and into a pouch at his belt. I made no move to stop him, merely watched as he refastened the strings and thrust the bulging purse under his jerkin.

"What news of the Velvet City?" Foo asked idly. Magrath froze in alarm and turned to stare at him warily.

"That's a wide question with too many answers," he muttered. "And too many ears, listening for them. They say," he went on, leaning forward in a conspiratorial manner, "the Council has found a way to tax even the dead. I know Black Wine is flowing in the cellars, but it's not coming down the river; I heard it sells well in Posmera these days. And the Veil was ripped open by the Duke himself when they tried to silence his Master at Arms. He don't like them meddling in his business. They won't forget that in a hurry."

"I daresay not," I remarked, turning his words over thoughtfully. Mugs does not deal in common rumour, but he's not adverse to passing it on without charge once more formal matters have been dealt with. I had already heard about the infamous 'coin of no breath' that Carthery's council had levied to pay for removing bodies from their streets. Nothing is illegal in the Velvet City, but many things require licenses and attract taxation, which is one way to keep the worst excesses from becoming too common. Since anyone fool enough to die in a Carthery street is promptly stripped and robbed of everything almost before they take their last breath, I doubted that this latest idea would raise much revenue. There would be little left for the tax collectors. Rumours of Black Wine were more interesting, although nothing to get too involved in if the trade was with Posmera; the subtle intoxicants used to turn simple grape juice into a powerful narcotic are rare and difficult to obtain. It enslaves anyone foolish enough to dare its exotic pleasures, and slowly rots the mind and body until nothing but corruption remains. As for the other business – well, if the servants of the Sable Veil were foolish enough to tangle directly with Duke Octian they deserved everything they got. The Sisterhood of the Veil is a poisonous contamination, one the Known Kingdoms would well do without.

I sighed, considering Magrath's wary face. The matter of Carthery was probably a question we should avoid exploring too deeply. If word of Alwick's diplomacy had escaped it would be a sufficient matter for coin, and I had no wish to pique any information broker's curiosity by offering it. "And what of the rest of the world?" I asked instead, finishing the contents of my goblet. "What tales of Greenhaven, or the isles of Endor? Does the Witch Queen still fret in her bone tower or has she directed her angers on to other things? Is there a new king in Farrikar? What word, Magrath?"

He shrugged, obviously relieved at the change of subject. He took another mouthful of his ale and paused to wipe his lips with the back of his hand. "Old tales, half heard rumours. If all you want is news, you want to catch a Troubadour. I hear about many marvels. I don't know the truth of any of 'em. I did hear as how the Stormholt has left Masren, but I don't know where he might be heading. Something has a taste for Hoomin sheep, up in the Down Country, but that might just be wolves. I'm told the House of Dalessandro has been trading old gold this season, and not from the Iron Heights either. And the Deep folk are watching their borders, it's said – keeping something in, not out. Strange lights have been seen over Oscallon, but that always happens this time of year. I've even heard it told that the Phaidor has been dead these five years past, and no-one noticed. What I'd want to know is as how you'd tell?"

"You'd tell," Foo muttered, his whiskers twitching at the thought. We had met Holden Tabbinor, Master of Esoteric Sciences and current Phaidor of Oscallon, not a year since, and a man more alive and certain of it would be hard to find. He fairly crackles with the power he commands, but despite that – and contrary to popular belief – he is both personable and approachable. Of course, he is an academic not a politician, but I consider that to be a benefit, not a failing. One of the letters I had found in Reinwald's study had borne Tabbinor's personal seal, although not his signature – a probable sign of our missing Archmagus's standing among his peers.

I thanked Magrath and he watched us leave, his nervous smile no doubt assuaged by another tankard of ale as soon as we had gone. The burly bartender scowled in our direction as we ascended the stairs; he probably thought I was some idle high born lady slumming for entertainment's sake. I wondered if Magrath would enlighten him. Foo favoured him with a menacing hiss which dissolved into a laugh as we emerged onto the narrow street and I frowned at him reproachfully. That only widened his grin.

"You can be a cruel lady," he considered affectionately. "If you'd asked, I would have fetched Magrath to the street to meet you. He trembled over much in there, I think."

"He trembles over much wherever I choose to meet him," I observed, gesturing him down the alleyway. "But at least I know he is reliable. And I didn't see you volunteering to save his sensibilities before we sat to drink."

"I was thirsty. And you were paying."

That deserved the hint of a smile. "So I was," I agreed softly. "So I was."

Chapter Eleven

The Paradoxican stands on the corner of Festive Square, less than a stone's throw from the Purchase Gate and opposite the Festival Fountain. We had run past it the day before while the bespelled dagger circled the tumble of its water. Perhaps I should have noted it then, the hesitation in the finding that spoke of time spent in that place, but we had been so close to our quarry that the thought had not crossed my mind.

The theatre is an old building, constructed of stone and brick at its base and bedecked with ornate timber framing above. It sprawls lazily around the corner of the square, one frontage offering an ornamented entrance into the public seating and the other providing a backdrop of painted scenes with plaster figures that cavort among them. The angled wedge that the cobbles of the square cut into the structure turns it into a part eaten pie; behind its painted main entrance the theatre is actually a circular construction, containing a tiered amphitheatre. Hoardings on the painted walls boast of over a thousand seats; certain regular performances can easily fill the place, particularly at festival time. The Paradoxican serves several small, semi-regular companies in the city, many of which have sponsors in the Inner City. Religious mystery plays are their main fare, performed on holy days appropriate to their themes, but historical and legendary subjects are generally more popular. Alwick occasionally commands a performance at court, although he prefers the less formal entertainment offered by travelling players.

There are three other theatres in Nemithia, but they are small and intimate compared to the Paradoxican. It boasts a roof of waterproofed parchment that allows performances to take place in practically any weather, and four magically primed lamps that burn as bright as day without heat or flame. The city owns it, and its manager is appointed by the Council of Prefects. I wondered if he knew who lurked beneath his stage.

Foo found the 'lowest door' round to one side, a shallow incline leading down to what seemed to be a cellar entrance of some sort. There were doors of all shapes and sizes in the curve of the theatre's rear wall, some large enough to admit a dragon, although I doubt any would choose to use it. This one was partially concealed by a grating that lay level with the street. The door itself was small and made of plain wood, set into a snug casement and pierced by a single shuttered window. The shutter was closed when we reached it, and the door seemed to be locked.

At this discovery I glanced at my companion thoughtfully. Foo is rarely hampered by the minor problem of locked doors, but we were here to meet with the mysterious Magpie, not sneak into his hiding place unannounced. Foo threw me a wry look, undoubtedly struck by the same thought. At my encouraging nod he reached forward and knocked gently against the shutter.

We waited while a gust of cold wind whipped around us, bringing the sharpness of returning rain. The sky was once again an overcast grey, the light muddying even the impudent colours that painted the exterior of the theatre. A gaggle of workmen hurried by in the street, their cloaks huddled tight against the wind; they were followed by a portly clerk being harassed by urchins, his protesting voice gruff over their childish taunts. Foo raised his hand to knock a second time but drew it back as the shutter snapped open and a pair of gleaming eyes peered out at us.

"Yes?" the voice demanded, high pitched but clearly masculine.

"We have business with the Magpie," I said softly. "Is he at home?"

The man behind the door peered at us suspiciously, his shape little more than a vague shadow seen through the small opening. Foo stared back, his nose wrinkling a little as he drew in a breath to taste the scents carried on the air. I kept my face impassive, my armour concealed beneath my cloak, and my hand on Dancer's hilt, just in case. After a moment or two the shutter was snapped shut again with a decisive slam.

"Well," Foo began to say, but was silenced by the sound of a bolt being drawn. It was followed by another, then another. Eventually, the door creaked open, just a crack.

"Just the two of you?" the voice asked suspiciously. "No Wardens, or Royal Livery?"

"Just us," Foo drawled, his tone implying that we were quite sufficient for anything. The door opened a little wider.

"You'd better come in," the voice suggested, still sounding suspicious. "And quickly."

We did just that, the door closing behind us with firm intent, sealing us inside a shadow-filled corridor. I heard the bolts being slammed into place with haste and saw Foo's eyes gleam as they quickly adjusted to the lack of light. Our host was a lanky shape in the murk and he scurried away down the passage, beckoning us after him. The route was cluttered, boxes stacked on either side, their parade punctuated by numerous closed doors; the floor sloped down quite steeply, and the passage curved round, so that our sight of the entrance was quickly lost. A R'rruthren has no problem seeing in semi-darkness but I was forced to walk cautiously in Foo's wake, relying as much on touch as on sight as we were led deeper into the bowels of the Paradoxican.

Abruptly we emerged into a much larger space, still cluttered and cramped by a multitude of shapes but with an open feel to it all the same. The floor levelled out, and there was a source of illumination somewhere ahead throwing odd silhouettes and shadows into our path: the leer of a lurking troll, the menace of grotesque claws, even the sinister gape of a horned drake loomed at us as we passed. They were not real. There were no sounds to enhance the illusion, no movement except for a gentle sway of shadow on shadow as our guide's passage disturbed the figures that cast such alarming shades. I had heard Foo draw in a wary hiss as the first such menace loomed out of the darkness, then his laugh as he realised what they were.

I lacked the advantage of dark-adjusted eyes, but knowing where we were was sufficient to tell me what amused him. The myriad of figures and other shapes that surrounded us were mere illusions, the painted images that would be employed to dramatic effect by players on the stage above our heads. Leering devils, carved demons, chiselled Stone Folk, even distorted dragons cavorted about us in total disarray. Giant puppets dangled from beams overhead, while fabric draped trees and painted stones paraded alongside more exotic snatches of landscape; in between were stacked crates and boxes overflowing with fakery. Our guide led us deeper into the maze of structures and devices, heading in the approximate direction of the distantly glimpsed light. We ducked under a half-built ship's bows, skirted constructions that made no sense whatsoever, and emerged unexpectedly into a sudden order amid the chaos.

The Magpie's nest was not what I would have suspected, given the nature of his surroundings. It was fronted by a canvas flat – a piece of stage scenery painted to resemble a stone wall and pierced by a portcullis in the centre of it. The light I had glimpsed was spilling through the fretwork, concealing whatever lay behind it. The man opened a concealed gate in the imposing grillwork and ushered us into the brightness beyond. Inside was a neatly ordered corner, equipped with assorted furniture that had been carefully aligned with precision, all the wooden surfaces polished and gleaming, and the bed smoothed with deliberate care. Heavy tapestries hung on three sides, with the canvas and its carved gate making up the fourth. I blinked and took a moment to let my vision readjust. The light was not torchlight, but the faintly chill glow of mage work, its typical purple tint throwing stark shadows onto the walls of gently rippling cloth.

Foo bounded across to tap at the enchanted lamp, throwing me a look as he did so. His nose twitched, but the low-level magic drew no further reaction from him. He needed no words to convey his thoughts; it was obvious that the Magpie did good business if he could afford such luxuries – if he'd paid for it, of course.

I glanced around the room within a room, seeing the woven shapes of hunting griffins chase across the fabric walls. The tapestries were crude and quickly woven, backdrops to some dramatic presentation rather than commissioned works of art. One was a hunting scene, another depicted a distant castle in a rocky landscape, and the third showed armoured knights combatting a beleaguered pair of manticores. All the figures were larger than life, brightly coloured and crudely drawn. Against that dramatic background the man himself was revealed to be a drab and understated figure – deliberately so, I might have said, since he was in a business where it does not pay to be very memorable. No doubt most of the Magpie's customers would pass him on the street without so much as a second glance, unrecognisable away from his theatrical setting.

I was not surprised to find that our guide was also the man we sought; he scuttled across to his desk and waved me to the seat beside it with respectful intent if not strict politeness. He was very nervous and showed it by wringing his hands distractedly as he dropped to the very edge of his chair where he perched a little like his namesake might – ready for flight at the first sign of alarm. I sat with care, letting a moment of silence relax the man's tensioned shoulders. Foo found a nearby perch on a solid looking storage trunk where he wrapped his tail around his feet and studied our quarry through lowered lids. The Magpie was not a young man. His hair was reduced to straggly wisps around a balding pate, his body lean and bony so that long limbs were exaggerated into awkward angles, while his shoulders were rounded over so that his head appeared to bob on a fluid neck that had difficulty coping with its weight. Thick-lensed glasses perched on his prominent nose, Kharad crystal by the look of them; they magnified the pale eyes behind them into watery orbs of wary alarm.

"Did you come to sell, or buy?" he questioned abruptly, tilting his head to consider both of us with a series of darted glances. His movements were decidedly birdlike, the impression aided by his apparent general fragility.

"That," I answered softly, "may depend on what you have to offer us."

His eyes narrowed behind the circles of crystal, and then unexpectedly, he smiled. "I could not afford your power, my lady," he said, dipping his head in amused embarrassment. "Not even put a price on it. I know men who would kill for one tenth of the fineness of the sword at your hip, and as for the other one…" He shuddered with exaggerated emphasis and Foo let out a chittering laugh that he smothered with difficulty. I decided to ignore him.

"You know me, Master Magpie?"

"Of you," he assured me quickly, glancing nervously at my companion as he did so. "I have – a gift, my lady. To witness the presence of power. It hangs about you like a second cloak, and I did not need to see the sword you carry to know that it was there. An armoured lady of the Light, companioned by a true son of the Hunter – there is only one in all of Asconar that you could be."

I studied him for a moment longer, then acknowledged the truth of his assessment with a small dip of my head and the hint of a cold smile. He relaxed visibly, still anxiously nervous but less inclined to flight. "It seems I have need to remember I have a reputation," I murmured, letting the fold of my cloak fall away so that the mage light glinted off my armour. The Magpie's eyes narrowed a little as he registered the faint gleam of the crystal at my throat, then widened when he realised that it had no chain to hold it there.

"To what – do I owe this honour?" he asked, his voice

pitched too high on the first words so that he was forced to pause and clear his throat.

"I have reason to believe," I considered, "that you may have possession of something I have been looking for."

He blanched. Behind their glass defenders, his eyes flicked this way and that, darting glances that served only to highlight the potential locations of his most valuable merchandise. It must have been the presence of My Lady that unnerved him so since I could not imagine that he would have survived so long in his trade if his normal business was conducted with so much indiscretion. On the other hand ... My own eyes narrowed a little as I leant forward in my seat and studied him more closely. He wore a twisted copper torque under the white linen of his collar, and an ornate amulet hung at his breast. His hand drifted to it, touching it briefly before he jerked his fingers away. "I am – protected – my lady," he gulped, the statement half warning, half swallowed fear. It was my turn to relax, my suspicions amply confirmed by his announcement. My Lady grants me a sense for the presence of power, but it takes effort and concentration and tends to only focus on the most active of sources. In this cramped space my sensitivity would undoubtedly have been misled by the presence of the Mage light, and I would not have been certain of what else lingered nearby. The Magpie's gift was obviously more focussed than my own, since that was the reason for his trading, but not even he could be certain that his carefully purchased defences would stand against my hand should I decide to act against him. If I had had Dispiriter at my back there would have been no doubts in the consideration.

I took pity on his anxiety, spreading my empty hands a little to illustrate my peaceful intent. "My Lady's hand is not raised against you, Master Magpie. I intend you no harm, nor will offer any if you deal with me truthfully. Tell me – why would a thief bring you a diamond, when you deal in power not price?"

Behind their circles of crystal his eyes narrowed down into shrewd consideration. His hands, which had been wringing each other nervously, stilled abruptly. "The two are not incompatible, my lady," he said. "Those things that men hold precious are often best for holding power, too. That may be why certain things survive from ancient times – because the ignorant value their surface price, even if unaware of what might lie within."

Out of the corner of my eye I saw Foo's ear swivel back, as if he had heard some subtle sound somewhere in the maze of props and puppetry. Since he made no further move, I paid the matter no attention. A place like the Paradoxican was probably crawling with rats. "And what might lie within a diamond?" I asked, cupping my fingers to demonstrate the size of the piece I sought. "Particularly one for which you paid so little, given what it might fetch from a dealer in such stones."

His lips pursed with disapproval. "It was not his to sell," he considered righteously. "I gave him coin to keep him from my throat, only promising more when it was sold on. Then I sent word to its owner." The corner of his mouth twitched with suppressed anxiety. "Did he send you?"

I avoided the question, countering it with one of my own. "You knew the piece?"

His head bobbed with nervous assent. "For certain," he replied. "'T'was I who bought it from that fool adventurer, these ten years since. I do not forget such things. It is rare that I encounter such a brilliant light, or so subtle an enchantment. Pre-Domination, at a guess. Some pretty toy to amuse a mover of mountains."

"As old as that. And still certain in its magics?"

"Diamond," he pointed out stuffily, "does not tarnish, my lady." A brief smile scuttled across his lips. "The Archmagus took six months divining its purpose and command. An orrery, he called it." Behind me, Foo jerked upright from his deceptive slump, a reaction echoed by our nervous host as something clattered noisily out in the darkened storage area. "Who's out there?" he called, his voice pitched high and anxious.

No answer echoed back from the cluttered store beyond the light. Foo rose into a tense crouch, his ears flattened back, his nose and whiskers twitching almost imperceptibly. My hand dropped to Dancer's hilt as the Magpie stared anxiously into the dark. "You said you came alone," he hissed, his head darting from side to side as he scanned the shadows beyond the grillwork.

"We did," I answered. Foo growled and padded to the portcullis door, pushing it open with a cautious hand. "Rats?" I hazarded, although I knew that was not the answer. The edges of the hanging tapestries ruffled as if a sudden gust of wind had stroked them into life.

"A man," Foo decided. "An anxious one." His claws flexed out as he reached to slide a knife from its sheath. "Keep talking." He slid out into the darkness with the fluidity of shadow, his furred feet making no sound on the wooden flooring.

"Probably a would-be thief," I suggested, motioning the Magpie to resume his seat.

"The entire city guild could search this place and not find a thing," he said, once again perching nervously on the edge of the chair. "But they know that well enough. And there is nothing in the theatre worth lifting when the stage is empty. For all that ..." He craned his neck anxiously, trying to see over my shoulder. "I am here to watch these things."

"The trade is just a sideline, then," I murmured, my own attention more directed towards noises in the dark than hearing his words. He laughed nervously.

"Say – a hobby," he suggested. "My gift is sure, but singular, my lady. I have no other talents for power, and my heart was always set towards the stage. Here I have the best of both persuasions."

"There is no fault in finding one's true place in life," I agreed softly. "As I well know. Tell me about the Star Diamond, friend Magpie. What is its power?"

His eyes were still fixed on the darkness beyond the circle of light. "You should ask its Master that, not I," he answered. "He did not give me its commanding words, nor would I ask them of him. I expected him to come for it before now."

"He cannot," I began to say, but got no further. Somewhere out in the darkness I heard Foo sneeze, an explosive protest of sound that echoed in the cavernous space beneath the stage. Behind my anxious host the garish hunting scene rippled into furious life. It was sudden and totally unexpected; one moment the cloth hung still and heavy, suspended from a series of polished brass rings; the next saw it curl up at the lower edge and lunge forward, like a striking snake or a hunting bird stooping for prey. The fabric strained against the rings which held it for a second then tore free, sending the metal rattling around the supporting rod. I sprang to my feet in alarm, giving the Magpie cause to turn and react just as the volume of cloth tumbled over him.

Emerald fire flared around the lanky figure, its light piercing the folds of cloth as it squirmed over and around him. The tapestry shivered like a living thing, intent on engulfing its chosen victim. The Magpie cried out, his voice muffled by the fabric. He fought to be free of its grip, the magical shield he had summoned pushing it into irregular bulges as he twisted under its weight. I started to slide Dancer from her sheath, then changed my mind and reached instead for the hunting knife that hung at my other hip. The tapestry twisted sideways, dragging the man within off his chair and tumbling him to the floor. The emerald light flared brighter before it was extinguished by the layers of cloth; I skirted the edge of the desk and grabbed the nearest fold, pulling the weight of the fabric towards me. It resisted, jerking away from my hand with a deliberate tug. The whole mass was squirming, the man within still struggling to be free.

"Lie still," I commanded, slashing at the cloth with the knife. Threads parted, the coarse weave giving before the sharp edge. I hacked off a largish piece and tossed it to one side, reaching for the next fold. The tapestry moved as I grasped at it, rolling and shifting in the confined space. Again I cut into its weave, the upward slash of the knife forcing its folds apart. The separated pieces simply tightened their grip.

Something flapped against my ankle, and I glanced down to find the first piece I had discarded trying to slither up my leg. The cut edges of the cloth were beating at my hands and the whole bundle was writhing tighter, intent on smothering the man it contained. Somewhere behind me fabric tore and metal rings rang out a note of warning. Darkness came with the impact of weight, a smothering darkness, musty and enveloping. I was dragged back and then over, tumbling into the desk as I did so. My arms were quickly enwrapped and immobilised, my struggles only serving to help complete my entrapment. The knife was pulled from my hand. Cloth folded over my head, only the coarseness of the weave saving me from immediate suffocation. I lay in the dark and felt the fabric begin to pull tighter, felt it twist and squirm against the barricade of my armoured body. A fold slid around my neck and began to pull taut.

Had I been other than I am I might have panicked then. The steady inevitability of my intended fate seemed inescapable. The Magpie's magical shield protected him, although I could not know how long that might last. Like the stone gargoyles I had fought not so long since, the single-minded purpose of the empowered fabric seemed unstoppable. It had been fire that had dispersed that earlier enchantment, although such a solution to my current plight would undoubtedly be as bad as the initial attack. But I have other strengths to call upon, although I rarely seek such aid except in desperate circumstances. I closed my eyes, stilled my breath, and began to pray.

It is not in my calling to beg aid for myself. Such selfish pleas would fall upon deaf ears and go unrecognised until such time as I stood for final judgement. But I might speak for other lives, and I did so now, committing my own soul into the hands of My Lady and begging her mercy for the beleaguered man who shared my fate. Such prayers are not always answered. The gods make their own judgements and it is not our lot to question them, only accept that our limited view is not enough to grasp the greater picture. Some powers even delight in capricious favours, granting one wish and denying another seemingly without reason or concern – but My Lady is merciful. I trust her, and her purposes. I have walked her path willingly since that cold day when I offered myself into her service. I cannot turn back, nor easily turn away, no matter what it cost me to stay the trail.

The cloth choked the words in my throat. Stars danced in front of my eyes. My heart thudded into silence, and all sensation drained from my limbs. The weight of the fabric seemed to melt away, leaving me entombed in ice. I could not breath, I could not move. For a long moment I was nowhere at all. Then silver fire flared into me, starting as a white hot point of sensation at my throat that quickly burned through every pore in my body. It consumed me utterly in barest seconds. Had I been able, I might have screamed.

Chapter Twelve

It was R'rruthren claws that ripped the heavy fabric off me. By then it was no more than inanimate weight, and the weave parted like paper under Foo's determined assault. I was too weak to help him. I lay and shivered while he lifted me out of the engulfing folds and placed me on the yielding surface of the bed. The Magpie hovered somewhere behind him, his angular features outlined by the magelight which seemed oddly dim after the assault of silver that still shimmered somewhere at the back of my vision.

"Give her a moment," I heard my friend say, distantly. "This will pass."

He was right. Strength flooded back slowly, like a returning tide washing over a storm-touched shore. Sensation returned with a tingling of muscles and skin where I had thought to be burnt to the bone. The crystal at my throat still pulsed softly, its light reflected in the gleam of Foo's eyes as he bent over me with concern. I found a smile of reassurance from somewhere and offered it with a dash of wry acceptance, a look he returned with clear relief.

"Is she all right?" The Magpie's voice was shaky but reassured me of his survival along with my own.

"Aye," Foo purred, leaning forward to polish at my breastplate with his forearm. "It is no easy thing to channel the power of the gods, but she bears it better than many do. You should offer prayers of thanks to her Lady. She thought your life worth saving, it would seem."

I had no need of such a reminder. My own acknowledgements of My Lady's mercy were already spoken, deep in my heart. The lanky figure behind my friend took off his glasses and polished them nervously on his sleeve. "I will," he promised, his head bobbing in birdlike embarrassment.

"I saw the light clear from the other side of this place," Foo told me, his whiskers twitching slightly. "Had I known you to be in peril ..."

"You did not know," I reassured him, easing myself upright. I was relieved to find that the room quickly ceased its sudden spin about me when I did so. "What word of our intruder?"

Foo's lip curled up into an expression of chagrin. "I near had him," he admitted slowly. "That is ..." He reached down and lifted up a handful of nothing from the floor. "I had his disguise."

The Magpie had replaced his glasses. Behind the circles of crystal his eyes widened in startled surprise. He had good reason. Foo's hand no longer appeared to spring from the end of his arm. Instead it was blurred into a confusion of light and darkness that slowly settled into nothing at all. I blinked, reached out my hand, and met resistance, hanging in folds of silk like fabric from the R'rruthren's non-existent grip. He laughed at my reaction and tossed his prize into my lap. The fabric was light weight and billowed open across my knees. Where it fell, the shapes it covered blurred then slowly vanished. I found myself bisected, sitting on an empty space and staring down at the floor beneath the bed

"It's beautiful," the Magpie breathed, crouching down to stroke at the non-existent fabric. "So full of light..."

"So full of nothing at all," I said, then glanced at him, realising what he had said. "You can see this?"

"I can," he murmured, his hand caressing the silk that only he could see. "Such workmanship. A Masterpiece. True Weaver's work – like your cloak, my lady."

My lips curled in the barest of smiles. "The Weaver who made my cloak would be flattered at the comparison," I said. "This is indeed a Masterpiece. Several years of work, I should think. Worth a fortune – and the answer to a thief's prayer."

"Only to human eyes," Foo snorted. "It did not mask his scent, or the sound of his heart and breath. A pretty toy though, and a useful one."

I turned the fabric over in my hand, feeling the cold touch of the woven silk slide through my fingers. True Weavers might work with light and power, weaving on their looms of living wood, but the skill to produce fabric made purely from light alone is a rare one indeed. Just as well, perhaps, or the world would be plagued by invisible thieves. "With such a thing," I considered, "an ambitious burglar might risk the wealthiest mansions in Nemithia. Perhaps even the palace. Why come here? "

"Because we had located something he wanted." Foo grinned, then let his lip lift into a snarl. "Willing to kill for it, too, I'd say. Those tapestries did not stir of their own account."

"Certainly not," the Magpie huffed, eyeing the ruin of his hangings with distaste. "That was purposed power – ill purposed, I would say. And the skill to place life in such things is as rare as the fabric he came cloaked in." He stared at the two of us suspiciously. "Which mage have you so offended that he would seek your end in such a way?"

"No mage," Foo answered decidedly. "A mage's man, perhaps, but no great wreaker of power, by all accounts of him."

I looked up from my study of the unseen cloak to frown at my companion's words. "You recognised him," I identified slowly. "Knew his scent?"

Foo nodded, his whiskers wrinkling with faint chagrin as he realised that he had omitted to tell me the most important information he had uncovered. "It was Eachan," he announced.

It was not the answer I had been expecting. The use of power in this affair had pointed me towards an over-ambitious apprentice, one who would know what minor items his master would not immediately miss, and one whose skill might stretch to the moving stone or the enlivened cloth. The bitter ex-warrior had not featured high in my suspicions despite, or perhaps because of, his hostile manner. "I can understand the cloak," I said, clenching my hand around the fabric, "since we already know that the Archmagus's goods are a part of this puzzle, but where would Eachan gain the power to move stone or cloth?"

"From the same place?" Foo hazarded, glancing at our host as he did so. "He didn't stop to cast any spells that I could see. But there was magic in the air. Perhaps he has some trinket or other that triggers such attacks." The Magpie's suspicious look had faded into one of puzzlement. At my comrade's words his face went stark white.

"An item?" he gasped. "Not a wreaking of will?" He sank to the nearest chair, pulling off his glasses to wipe at his brow. "I was wondering how such power could be so undirected. Workings like that take great concentration to effect – even when the spells are stored within a talisman."

"But items do exist that allow such things to happen," I prompted, wondering why he was so shaken by the thought.

"Oh, yes," he agreed weakly. "That is – I've heard things ..." He took a careful breath to steady himself and paused once again to polish his lenses before he replaced the framework on his nose. "Let me explain," he said, blinking owlishly behind his crystal shields. "There are laws that govern the use of power. Just as there are seven recognised branches of Magecraft, so there are also seven defined categories into which items of power can be placed. Some are more commonly encountered than others, of course, and certain items can be classified in more than one category – like the craft, the divisions are not exact."

Foo's ears rolled back in resignation. It was obvious we were in for a lecture on a subject we already knew fairly well, but I laid my hand to his arm to silence the threatened comment and nodded for the man to continue. I was interested in his conclusions, although I had a strong suspicion as to what they were going to be. More importantly, his nerves seemed to drain from him as he held forth; I wanted him calm and steady.

"There are two areas where the mage has no influence and those are that of the Holy Relic, and the gifts of the gods." He smiled a little nervously at me as he said this, and I suppressed the temptation to touch the crystal at my throat. "Those aside," he continued, "the most common type of item is that enchanted to retain a given spell or spells – such as this." He hefted the amulet he still wore. "Once triggered, the power is used and cannot be reused, unless recharged in some way. Next is the item whose enchantment is some type of enhancement – the sword that never grows dull, the bag that holds more than it should, and so on. Then we have enpurposement, of which there are two types – the first that affects the wearer or holder, rather than the item, and the second that affects the item itself. Sixth is the item that is magic in itself – such as my light, or this cloak. And last comes the device designed to empower other things without itself or its wielder being affected."

He was well into his stride now, and there was less of a shake in his voice. "All things that might be found, or made, or empowered will fit one or more of these categories. Most will be of little power and smaller consequence, of course. Some, however, can be items of great power indeed – and they can be dangerous even in experienced hands. Magic is a craft, not a science, and no one item is ever exactly the same as any other, since they always carry the stamp of their maker. Many," he added pointedly, "demand a price for their use."

Foo's eyes narrowed down into wary slits. "All of which is interesting…" he began to say. I silenced him a second time.

"Items in the last category more than any other?" I suggested, keeping my voice mild. The Magpie nodded vigorously.

"Exactly. If you create something to empower something else then you either have to set a limit to it – so that when all the power placed in the item is transferred it ceases to function – or you require some other input of power in order for the transference to take

place. Only the gods can create energy out of nothing."
He sighed, probably only too aware of how my Lady had
saved his life.

"So the process of bringing something unliving to
life …" I began.

"… probably requires an input of life to do it," the
talismonger concluded, suppressing a shudder with a
nervous laugh. "That's a dangerous practice at the best
of times. A transference of will returns to its originator
when concentration is broken. But this enchantment was
worked without concentration at all …"

"Teeth of the Underwolf," Foo hissed, "I thought I
smelt blood on him!"

"Some small animal?" the Magpie suggested hopefully.
The R'rruthren shook his head.

"No. His own."

I drew in a sharp breath, while the Magpie went even
whiter than before. His hands groped for the amulet at
his breast, an automatic gesture since its protection had
now been discharged. "Do such fools exist?" he asked in
a strangled tone, and I nodded, understanding his alarm.

"Perhaps he does not know what he risks," I hazarded.
Foo hissed quietly.

"Then he is twice a fool," the Magpie decided. "Magic
is not a toy and blood magic is always dangerous. Using
your own life to give life – such a thing is not lightly
undertaken.   But to use such things without
understanding the cost – that is sheer folly. It won't be
just a blood price this thing demands, but a piece of his
own self. His soul, or his life in some manner."

"Are you sure?" Foo asked, his eyes narrowing warily.
The talismonger nodded.

"Quite sure. There was no focus behind that attack –
only a directive. If he used an item to bestow this effect
then once he gave the tapestries life there would be no
way of taking it back."

I fingered the invisible cloth thoughtfully. "To do such
a thing once," I considered, "might be worth the risk.
Such costs are recoverable over time."

The talismonger eyed me owlishly behind his circles of crystal. "Time may be the essence," he said. "Sometime the price of such things is measured by the passage of it – a year from your life can be a worthwhile sacrifice to some."

Foo snorted. "If that is the truth of it," he growled, "then I would look to see grey hairs in the man's head. Twelve stone carvings he stirred yesterday – and two lengths of cloth today. "

"So much?" The Magpie blinked in disbelief. "Then it is not years he pays with but something more. He must be paring away his very self without knowing it."

"The price of power is always high," I murmured, my hand drifting to the crystal at my throat. "But what do you gain if, by paying for it, power is all you have?"

The bleak look in the Magpie's eyes was all the answer he needed to give.

**

"I still don't understand," Foo growled unhappily as we made our way back through the Inner City towards Kellmarch House, "why Eachan is so eager to reclaim the diamond, and why he is willing to risk so much to get it."

"Neither do I," I answered grimly. "We shall have to ask him." My companion glanced at me warily, and then shuddered.

"You don't have to do this," he pointed out. "We could raise all the Lions to our aid if we needed them."

That brought a brief flicker of amusement to my lips. "And have Alwick think me incapable of attending to my own business?" I shot back. "Beside leaving the King undefended."

"Aye, well," he admitted. "But you know what I mean."

I drew to a halt and turned to regard him with patient affection. "Foorourow Miar Raar Ramoura," I said, "I understand your concerns for me. But I can no more change what I am than you can grow Hoomin horns on your furred head. This business has gone beyond simple

169

matters of the sword. He has used power to kill and used it without thought or regret. I cannot willingly choose to expose others to such chances unless I am sure that I do not have the strength to face him."

"And you have the strength," he admitted, his whiskers drooping unhappily. "I know. It is just that … this whole business has me jumpier than a kitten on his first hunting. Disappearing Mages, statues and tapestries that move of their own accord, crippled warriors sneaking about in shrouds of nothing … and you want to bring – you know – into it."

"I have to," I told him sternly. "I want answers, and I want Eachan stopped before he brings harm to innocent folk. If it hadn't been for Kirby and Stonecutter I would not have held my own against those gargoyles, and if it hadn't been for My Lady just now …"

He threw up his hands in accepting surrender. "You act as you must," he said. "I only serve as your shadow."

"My anchor, you mean." I put my hand to his shoulder and he dipped his head to rub his cheek along my arm. We are old friends and his concern reassures me. He fears that I might lose my humanity under the burden I must bear, and while he holds those fears I know that I have not done so.

"We are wasting time," he reminded me, sliding from under my hand to pounce along the street. A figure wrapped in a leather cloak hurried past, sparing the two of us a brief glance before turning his head back into the wind. We had chosen back streets for speed, and the narrow alleys funnelled the autumn air into a biting impact that kept all but the hardiest or the needful from braving it.

"We are indeed," I agreed and strode on, the impact of my armoured heels ringing against the cobbles. The wind tugged at the edge of my cloak, shivering its tiny bells; beneath it I carried both the fine weave of the unseeable fabric and the cold weight of the Star Diamond. The Magpie had been more than glad to relinquish both into my care.

The diamond certainly lived up to its reputation. It was a flawless gem, easily the size of a hen's egg, cut into a myriad of facets that reflected light in a multitude of colours. Deep in its heart lay a miniature sun, encircled by beads of brilliance. In my hand it hummed softly with the impact of its power; it was easy to see why Usurus had brought it to a talismonger rather than a gemcutter. Understand too, perhaps, why Eachan might seek it with a passion strong enough to kill in cold blood. I had not yet discovered its secret. I could not be certain that the injured warrior knew it, but I had cause to hope that he might. Somehow, I was sure, the fate of Reinwald lay tangled with the silent gem.

At Kellmarch House I sent Foo to fetch my repaired helm while I composed myself to climb the tower steps. The autumn sunlight slanted low through the range of windows below the tower roof and glinted off the silvered steel that lay on my altar stone. I knew, as soon as I set foot within the room, that I had been right in my decision. Her presence enfolded me with welcoming certainty. Foo may fear the effect her touch has upon me, but I have learned to accept it – to embrace it with determination. I cannot regret the choice I long ago faced; once the offer was made and the price accepted, my path had been carved before me in steps of steel and stone. I walk it with surety, with no regrets nor second thoughts.

I knelt before the altar before I took up my blade. The calm of My Lady's presence settled around me, filling me with strength and balance. It is a balance I need to bear her gift, and I accepted it without question. A moment longer steadied my heart and then I reached to claim what is mine alone.

I am changed when I carry Dispiriter's weight openly at my back. I walk with a certainty that few can refute or even face. I rarely need to wield her in combat, since her presence alone can lend me a power that can cow the most stubborn of hearts. My Lady's gift will not harm me, but other mortals have reason to fear, for her barest

Penelope Hill and J.A. Mortimore

kiss can cut clean to the soul; she was placed on this earth to face darker things than most men can imagine. When I ride the world, I wrap her in silks and hide her silver from the sunlight. This time I took her up with intent, leaving her uncovered at my back. Dispiriter is as light as silk when I carry her that way, despite the weight and heft of her blade. She has no sheath, just a simple chain that holds her in place at my shoulder, and which guards her point at my hip. I slipped that over my head and settled it in place, then lifted my sword over my shoulder, offering her to the chain. She claimed her accustomed place with a familiar touch; with it came the cloak of her power, an armour that guards me against magical or spiritual attack. Thus prepared, I turned and made my way down the waiting stairs.

The sense of her presence moved with me, leaving the quiet room empty of its silences.

Chapter Thirteen

Ravens Hill was cloaked in the shadow of rain as we made our way up the shallow steps towards Reinwald's house. The guard on Medrick's gate scurried to let us through, swinging the wooden door wide so that I had no need to slow my pace as we passed. Foo loped at my left side, watching the day-to-day activities of the city stumble to a halt as our parade of two swept past. People stepped aside without being asked, some openly gawping but most lowering their heads in unspoken respect. I ignored them all.

The house seemed quiet in the growing dusk, its gates open but its doors shut. The griffin rose from its crouch by the wall to screech once in our direction. Then it whined and slunk back to its kennel, wings tucked in and tail drooping. Foo scampered past to hammer on the door as I approached it. It opened, revealing a startled Theda who took one look at my face and dropped into a wary curtsey.

"My lady?" she queried, still bent at the knee. I considered her with calm intent, weighing her innocence and finding her untainted by anything other than petty impatiences and unspecified alarm.

"I have come for Eachan," I stated, my voice gentle but commanding. Her startlement turned to wide-eyed exclamation.

"How did my lady know ...?" she flustered in total astonishment. From somewhere above us there came an unnatural clatter followed by a cry of absolute terror. I strode past Theda's distraught reaction and made for the stairs, my companion at my heels. We met Mac Doonin at the second turn, his arms encumbered by the slumped form of a fellow apprentice, his face creased with anger and undirected power boiling about them both. Foo sneezed violently, turning the young man's head and I threw up my hand as lightning lanced between us.

The expended spell dissipated harmlessly in a flare of brilliance, its caster forced to shield his eyes from its disruption. He lowered his arm slowly and blinked at me with wordless confusion. The figure he supported was Deckle. Blood was bubbling from rips in the younger man's robe and staining them both. Somewhere behind us Theda let out a low moan of horror at the sight.

"I – I'm sorry my lady," Mac Doonin stuttered. "I didn't know…" His knees buckled. Foo stepped past me to support the pair, his ear flattening back in anger as he helped lower the injured youth to the polished wood. Relieved of his burden, the Endorian found the strength to straighten a little, even smiling briefly at the housekeeper where she cowered at my back.

"Help him," I commanded, sparing her less than a glance. "What befalls here, Mac Doonin?"

"Eachan," he coughed, leaning on Foo's proffered shoulder with obvious relief. "He has gone mad, or worse. He came home like one possessed and dragged young Hal up to the Master's study. When we made to follow him," he was gasping with exhaustion, a sign of strength expended with his power, "he set the sphinxes on us …"

My head jerked up, abandoning his weary face for the prospect of the upper landing and what might descend from there. I had wasted too much time before returning to this house, and by doing so might have cost an innocent his life. My hand reached to the hilt at my shoulder and Dispiriter slid into my grip as if she and I were one. "Stay here," I said softly. "I do not think I will be long."

Wooden guardians roamed the upper floor, carved figures wrenched from their silent vigil on the study doors. Smoke curled from one of them, evidencing how the apprentices had sought to defend themselves with conjured fire. Both of them clattered to the attack as I mounted the last few steps, their wings fluttering uselessly in two dimensional displacement. I let them come, planting my feet firmly on the top step, the blade held back at my shoulder. I might have seemed an easy target but I had no desire to prolong my delay.

The first leapt directly at me, its wooden claws extended and its mouth open in a silent snarl. My hand pulled down as I turned to let it pass, Dispiriter's edge slicing through the grain of the wooden neck almost without resistance. I felt the creature's borrowed life flicker away but did not stop to watch as what remained shattered and splintered the stair rail below me. Instead I completed my move with an easy step that brought me to the upper floor and turned to face the second menace as it careened in my direction.

Another simple step and sweep left lifeless wood clattering onto the floorboards. There are few powers in the Known Kingdoms that can match the silvered kiss of my blade; with Dispiriter in my hand I rarely have cause to waste breath or effort in prolonged combat. My Lady's presence inspired me as I stalked down the passageway, the crystal at my throat painting the air around me with a bright, white light. There had been blood on the second creature's claws and a child's terror pulled me with more certainty than any rope might have done.

Eachan was stood waiting by the study's outer door, the coldness of the outside air hanging around him. His face was deathly pale. Hal Markstele lay huddled at his feet, held there by an arrogant boot and his own distraught fears. The boy appeared unharmed, but blood was trickling down the exposed length of the man's crippled arm, its stain clear on the tip of the dagger he held in the other hand.

"I knew you'd come," Eachan hissed as I strode through the opening left when the sphinxes had obeyed him. There was a wild gleam in his eyes that spoke eloquently of madness. I narrowed my own and considered him, lowering the point of my blade to the floor. The Magpie had been right. Whatever device he had employed to inspire life to the lifeless had commanded a high cost. I was looking at an empty shell,

175

drained of direction and inspiration. Bitterness filled him, as if each emptying of self had allowed its poison to spread deeper into his soul.

"There is no need of this," I said, letting the presence I carried flow into my voice. If rationality remained to him he might not be beyond my reach. He winced, as if my words were blows.

"Do not think you can persuade me," he growled angrily. "Your gods have no mercy for me. They never did. They refused me my skill and now you would steal away the power I have earned."

"You do not know what you are doing," I warned him. "All power has a price and you pay too dearly for little gain."

"It's mine!" His cry was incensed. "Do you think I don't deserve it? Three long years shovelling horse-shit and being laughed at behind my back? He took me in from pity, not friendship. Worked me like a dog and promised me a mastery he had no intention of giving me. All I wanted was a little respect. A little control. So I took it. He's not laughing now, is he?"

"I don't know," I answered. I was uncertain of my course now I had arrived. It was death that I held in my hands and I had no desire to wield it until it proved needworthy. Eachan's madness came from power ill-used and hatred ill-directed. There would be no reasoning with him since his path was set, not by rational belief but by twisted suspicion.

"No," he smiled suddenly. "You don't, do you? You don't know where he is, even now." There was sneering triumph in his tones. "Else he would be here and not you at all. I'm the only one who knows. I watched and I waited and I learnt the word. And without the word all your chasing and stumbling goes to naught. So I win after all."

"Nobody wins, Eachan." I took half a step closer, lifting my free hand to point at the boy. "Let the child go free. He is of no worth to you."

"No," he snapped, lifting the bloodied dagger and

jabbing it in my direction. "I need him. To read me the words. To show me the power in things."

So that was it. Reinwald had thought to teach his wounded friend a smattering of power to compensate for his loss, only Eachan had had no talent for it – and his failure had twisted his bitterness into resentful action. Without the skill to study the workings of others or the ability to sense the subtleties of magical energies his mage-craft would be as crippled as his sword arm. No doubt he saw in the boy a chance to correct those failings; but young Hal had to have talent or else Reinwald would not have wasted time in his teaching. Even if he swore to serve his new master, his life would only hold for the time it took for Eachan to realise that he would soon be out measured. Fear and suspicion would destroy them both.

"I cannot let you go," I decided softly. "You have stolen that which you cannot control, and you have used it to wreak harm without concern for anyone it affected."

"Usurus deserved to die," he hissed. "He was a greedy fool and he thought he could cross me."

"And the people in the square?" I questioned, risking yet another half step forward. "Had Kirby and I not been there to hold them, those gargoyles would have attacked the crowd for certain."

"Their gods would have protected them." The irony was heavy, laced with bitterness. "Nobody is innocent, my lady. Not even you." The dagger jerked sideways, drawing a fresh line of blood from his already damaged arm. "And we have talked long enough."

"Don't be a fool," I cried, realising what he intended. Too late to stop him, even if mere words could have done so. The hand that held the dagger turned, dragging the ring he wore through the scarlet of his life. I saw the strength pulled out of him by the gesture. An almost casual motion threw the gathered power at its intended target but then he gasped and staggered back, not expecting it to have taken so much. It had been scarce minutes since he had given life to the sphinxes; without chance to recover that first gift, his second had cost him dearly.

Across the room, the stone dragons began to stir.

Eachan glared at me with triumphant hatred. "Kill her," he commanded, his voice rasping with effort. I spared him a glance before I turned to take a defensive stand. His face, already white, was deathly pale now, and the dagger had tumbled from nerveless fingertips. Still he watched with eager expectation, almost without awareness of his own distress.

Stone uncoiled from stone. The carved figure of the Celestial Sun tumbled free to shatter on the tiled floor beneath it. Chiselled claws reached down to impact into the ceramic patterning. Slowly, as if they had all the time in the world to complete their task, the sinuous door wardens reared back and disentangled themselves from their ancient duty. Craggy jaws opened in silent challenge as they dragged themselves towards me. Their twisted carving had been impressive work, but I doubted that their sculptor had ever envisaged them moving in three dimensions. Back legs were too short, wings too dumpy and pushed to one side: they were flattened parodies of the real creature, but they moved with directed intent and menace.

I backed away a little, putting space between the sweep of my blade and the fragile lives I had to protect. Eachan chuckled, thinking me afraid to face his creations.

One long table cracked and collapsed as the weight of stone overwhelmed it. The carved dragon staggered in the resultant wreckage, and its brother launched itself to attack.

I wasn't there when it landed.

I had learnt well from my encounter at the Spinner's temple. Sheer weight would advantage my opponents and their single-minded intent would brook no pause from mere injury. I dived forward as it did, dropping into a low roll and bringing the length of my gifted sword across its exposed belly. The edge bit, sending a momentary jar along the length of my arms, and then its power drove it home, cutting through solid stone with scarce hesitation. Dispiriter's stroke cut the creature in two, and Eachan screamed.

I could not tell if it were with pain, or rage. Nor could I spare the time to check. The wounded dragon creaked to a distressed halt as I regained my feet, its head extended in startled surprise. Its tail lashed once, toppling its second half to the floor, and then the whole thing shattered into splintered dust, sundered by forces it could not contain.

The second creature had clambered onto a sturdier table, giving it some height to attack. It snapped at my shoulder, its carved teeth striking sparks from my pauldron. I spun, parrying the reaching talons with automatic reaction. Stonecutter would have severed the reaching claws and sent them tumbling; Dispiriter's cold fire shattered them as they fell.

My opponent reared back, shrieking silently in accompaniment to its master's anguished cries. The movement gave me the opening I needed. My blade swung back in an easy motion, slicing through one wing and across the dragon's exposed chest, releasing the stolen life within. My head turned automatically as stone dust splintered around me. When I looked back, nothing remained but shattered debris.

Eachan was sobbing. With distress, not rage. I turned in his direction, returning my Lady's gift to its place behind my shoulder as I did so. The crippled swordsman was crumpled against the wall of windows, clutching at his chest and stomach. Blood oozed from under his hands, each wound a match to the blows I had inflicted only moments before. I caught back an exclamation and ran to his side.

I had no hope of saving him. His last casting had tied his life too strongly to his creations.

And Dispiriter's kisses do not heal.

They strike to the soul and deeper, cutting the threads that bind life to this earthly existence. Even if I had the strength – the will – to close the gaping wounds and staunch the blood they birthed, I could not have helped him. His spirit hovered between this life and the next, pulled by forces no man can in the end resist.

"I always knew," he gasped, "that I would die by the blade. Tell me. Do the gods exist?"

"They do," I answered. His mouth quirked in a bitter smile.

"Good," he managed, blood bubbling between his lips. "Then I can curse them when I come to judgement ..."

He died with a shudder and a jerk, twisted by anger and still fighting his destiny. He had never accepted the changes that had come to him, resenting the loss of his gift rather than thanking fortune for sparing his life. I watched what remained of his spirit step away, his arm still twisted and useless even in death. His wound had run deep, inflicted by self-hatred and fuelled by internal anger. I prayed that the gods, whichever of them chose to receive him, would be merciful.

Foo tells me that bearing my holy blade tends to make me cold. He may be right. I did not weep for Eachan, nor wish that I was able to. My sorrow for his death would come later, when the weight of my destiny was far from my hand and my mind, and it would come without threat of tears. He had killed without remorse, striking out at those he felt had wronged him. Like any warrior, he had been trained to kill, but surely only in defence and never with intent to harm the innocent. Had he retained the skill of which he had been so proud would he still have blood on his hands? I had no way to know. It is no easy thing to lose something you consider precious; harder still when it appears to be an injustice. But worst of all is choosing to deny that loss, refusing to move on and seeking to dwell forever in the past. Eachan had committed that particular sin and it had destroyed him. I do not look back – except in moments of quiet understanding.

I reached down and closed his eyes, bidding his ghost to pass on to judgement. He would have no chance to linger in the halls of death. Dispriter's release is always a certain one.

***

Young Markstele was unhurt but clearly greatly shaken by the day's events. He'd managed to retreat to the Archmagus' bedroom while I was fighting the dragons, and I told him to stay there while Foo went to fetch the housekeeper for me. I had not been at all surprised to find my faithful friend waiting in the doorway when I rose to my feet. It takes much more than a short command to keep him from my side when danger threatens. While he departed on the errand I walked across the room to stare down at the remains of my handiwork.

Stone chips littered the laboratory, most of them little more than dust. A carved horn or a chiselled scale were all that was left of the sinuous stone with which a madman had thought to destroy me. Dispiriter hummed quietly at my shoulder, content with her dispensing of justice. I was not. My purpose here had not yet been fulfilled and the progress of events still lacked one final conclusion to bring my tasks to an end.

I sighed and walked into the octagonal room behind the gaping archway that the dragons had been carved to protect. The stone pillar and the cushion it supported still stood silently at its centre. I reached behind my breastplate and drew out the cause of all the struggle in the past few days. The Star Diamond.

It nestled in my palm, light glinting from within it. In the darkened space behind the shattered stonework it was easier to see the tumble of stars and planets that it contained at its heart. Reinwald's orrery. The miniature sun at its centre glowed with brilliance while our world and its dual companions continued a slow dance around it. Suddenly, looking at it and the pattern of stars drifting within it, I had the answer to my puzzle. It was so simple, and so obvious that I began to laugh.

I was still laughing when Foo came back.

"By the Dancer," he exclaimed in some astonishment, "is the man's madness infectious?"

"No," I told him, sobering with ease. Theda was staring at me, Mac Doonin and the pale faced Deckle close behind her. The younger apprentice's wounds appeared to have been less life-threatening than I'd first thought, although he was clearly still in pain. I placed the diamond carefully on its waiting cushion and strode out of the tiny room with easy steps. "I just know where Reinwald is."

"The Master?" Mac Doonin echoed, the strain of recent conflict still clear in his eyes.

"Who else?" I questioned lightly. My Lady's favour still held me, the sword at my shoulder cloaking me with her power. I reached out and brushed Deckle's weary cheek, letting some of that strength flow into him. He gasped as the healing touch cascaded through his tired form. I ignored his stuttered thanks and accepted the length of silk that Foo silently offered to my hands. With it I enwrapped my burden and my strength, letting its power settle into brooding sleep. When I replaced Dispiriter at my shoulder my Lady's presence faded away and I found I was weary to my bones.

"I had the answer all along," I explained, knowing I needed to do this one last thing before succumbing to the shaking that was threatening to consume me. I had barely strength enough to contain it, and I knew that doing so would cost me, but I also knew that it would pass. It always did. Foo's hand brushed my arm and I threw him a brief glance of reassurance. This time the price had not been high. "It was Jarman who told me, although his words made no sense at the time. He had had the word from Reinwald himself. Through the mirror," I added at the looks this elicited. Theda shook her head in confusion and bustled away to sweep up the youngster who was watching us from the bedroom door. She did not even glance at the sprawled corpse beside the windows.

"Your master has Prince Broderick to thank for his freedom," I announced, turning to look back at the diamond and its resting place. "Were it not for his precipitous tampering with power, this matter would have remained a mystery for a long time."

"I don't understand," Deckle admitted. "Where is the master? What did Eachan do?"

"He closed a door," I said. "No more than that. But all of Reinwald's power serves him naught whilst he remains behind it. Eachan sought to be rid of him, but dared not risk his death. He feared him. But once he had imprisoned him, he feared his release even more. That is why he sought so hard to retrieve the Star Diamond. Why men had to die rather than allow it to fall into my hands."

"The diamond?" Mac Doonin realised, turning to stare at it in wary comprehension. "He's inside the diamond? But – there would be a word, or something. None of us would know it ... and Eachan is dead."

"I know." I considered wearily. "But we do have the answer. Reinwald himself supplied it before the mirror broke. Lord Jarman heard it and made no sense of it. He is a herald, though, and a good one. He reported what he heard faithfully enough."

I completed my half turn, taking up a careful stance before the shattered doorway. I knew I was right, although I had no idea how the miracle would be worked. Foo was watching me curiously. Reinwald's apprentices glanced at each other and shrugged their mystification. My expression was calm, although I was fighting the exhaustion that threatened to claim me. I asked My Lady for just one moment more.

"NOVA!" The word rang out with firm authority.

And suddenly the space before us was filled with stars.

Chapter Fourteen

"So what happened then?" Scarll asked, leaning forward in his chair with interest. Foo grinned.

"Well," he said, "Reinwald staggered out looking much as you might expect after being trapped in nowhere for a few days and proceeded to berate all and sundry about the state of his workshop, and how long it had taken us to find him and what he was going to do when he got his hands on Eachan ..."

The Prince of the House of Scarlet tipped back his head and roared with laughter. We were warmly ensconced in front of our fire at Kellmarch House, the crackle of the burning wood driving back the bitter howl of the wind outside. Autumn was giving way to winter with a vengeance, sharp storms coming down from the Midendras hills and fitful winds tunnelling along the Medlure valley. Scarll had been swept in by such a wind, Maris in tow – the pair of them bundled up in what seemed to be endless layers of wool – and proceeded to invite himself in for the evening. I had not seen him since that day in the palace gardens, the King's business taking him out of the city for a while, and he had asked for the whole of the tale in exchange for the excellent bottle of Chryskaan that he had brought with him. We would have told him anyway, but a Daberon likes to think he has bargained for his benefit and feels uncomfortable when receiving anything for free. The Merchant's obligation is ingrained deeply in the man's soul, and if I can avoid it, I know better than to abuse his sense of debt.

The Chryskaan was of the finest quality, Elfin brewed and imported from Greenhaven. It was honeyed nectar compared to what we'd been served at the Bolt and Pallet, a snippet of information that Scarll found very interesting indeed. He told us that he'd acquired the bottle when bartering over Phraif silk somewhere on the borders between Asconar and the Iron Heights. A minor diversion he'd become entangled in on his way back from Towerstele, he said, although it wasn't clear why he and the rest of Prince Rufus' company would have chosen to visit the borderlands so late in the year. It would have saved both time and effort to charter a boat to bring them back along the Medlure. He did mention something about the Prince's horse, and a bet – and then distracted us with a promise of news about Alwick's meeting, which he knew all about of course. But he insisted on hearing the tale of the vanished mage before he would even speak of it.

I'd sat Scarll down before my fire when he arrived, sending Maris down to join Garrick where I knew he'd be well treated. Delph had brought out the crystal glasses for the liquor, and Bej had sent up a veritable feast of fresh baked biscuits, herb bread and other palatables – enough to tempt even the most replete to taste just another mouthful. Foo had chosen his usual place on the rug, and shuffled into relaxed comfort, tail tucked neatly away, one hand free to snake food from his plate of titbits, the other curled around his glass, while I had sunk into the opposite chair and begun the tale for which the man had come.

The fire leapt in easy abandon, throwing bright shadows over our company. I hesitated over how much I should speak of the Magpie, but Scarll knew of him, which didn't surprise me in the least. He leant forward eagerly as I spoke of the chase through the city, shuddered at the description of the gargoyles, and drew in a sharp breath as the tapestries leapt to the attack. Scarlettini is a good audience for a tale, and good company when he forgets to wear the more dandyish of his masks.

"I take it you enlightened him as to the man's condition?" he asked once he had stopped laughing.

Foo rolled over onto his back and jabbed a claw in my direction. "She took full responsibility for everything," he yawned.

"I had promised to do so." My answer was defensive, but honest enough. I had sworn to explain to the Archmagus, and I had. He had been gruff but eventually grateful, frowning down at the wounds his erring servant had taken and carefully recovering the ring that had enabled the man to perform such mischief.

"It's a mistake," Scarll grinned over his glass, "taking responsibility. Deny everything, that's my motto."

"Everything?" I queried, and he laughed once again.

"Well – perhaps not *everything,*" he admitted, sharing a wicked grin with Foo. "But anything you can safely blame on somebody else."

I sighed. "You are a reprobate and a scoundrel, Scarll Scarlettini," I told him severely, "and the gods will judge you when you are called to account."

Foo's tail was quivering, and his whiskers twitched as he rolled back to snatch another titbit from his plate. "He'll match the Bargainer bid for bid, this one," he yowled happily. "Or sneak into heaven with a Hoomin's horns on his head. Some men are not destined for their just rewards."

"Speaking of just rewards," Scarll enquired, pouring himself another splash of the liquor, "just what did happen to young Broderick and his caravan?"

"Oh," I answered airily, "nothing they didn't deserve. Alwick made them pay for the mirror – a commission to Oscallon, I believe, although it will be a good year or more before Reinwald sees anything from that."

"Or in that," Foo grinned. I pushed at him with my foot and he lashed out at me with a friendly swipe of sheathed claws.

"And Reinwald himself set them all to learning the Phairfaneffra Declarations," I added. "Verbatim."

Scarll winced. "All of them?" He shuddered. "In Gespian?"

Foo shook his head. "In Skitaash." His throat and lips were not designed to master the click and whistle of the Phraif tongue, but he managed their name for it fairly well, considering.

Scarll shuddered with even more feeling. "That," he declared, "is not punishment, but torture. Young Broderick will be beggared for the year to come – was that not enough?"

"Reinwald did not think so," I answered primly, then allowed myself a small smile. "I think you may find it did not cost the prince as much in gold as might be suggested. The Queen is very fond of her son."

Our visitor grinned. "As are we all," he acknowledged softly, offering a toast to the flicker of the fire. "Queen Sharasaan," he said, and the three of us drank to her with respect.

"So what of your news?" Foo requested, bounding up to refill his goblet. "Did Reinwald make no comment on his experience while attending on the King?"

"He did not," Scarll shot back, eyeing the R'rruthren archly. "But what makes you think I have been in Alwick's company to know? I have been hunting with Prince Rufus in Towerstele and buying ribbon in Moderain to gift my butterflies."

"Because," Foo answered, not at all put out by the man's reaction, "we know you, Scarll Scarlettini. You turn up in two places at once and are always in the middle of intrigue."

The prince glanced at me for support, but I merely considered him patiently over the rim of my glass and he sighed. "Very well," he allowed reluctantly, then broke into a broad grin. "You do know that Alwick came down with a cold and fever and was confined to his bed for a while?"

"Of course I know," I said, keeping a straight face with ease. "I was called upon to attend him several times." Scarll looked startled and Foo laughed.

"The Queen plays a good hand at Hunt and Scurry," my R'rruthren explained with relish. "It was lucky we were only betting sweetmeats."

"I do not gamble for gold," I pointed out, since our visitor was considering him with a frown of astonishment. Scarll blinked, glancing between the two of us, then chuckled warmly.

"Of course you don't," he said. "And I know the Queen's skill at cards – I have played her myself on occasion."

"Letting her win?" Foo enquired sweetly, and the prince threw back his head and laughed with delight.

"Aye," he admitted. "As you did, whiskerbreath. She would not know how your tail gives you away."

I hid my reaction to that behind the rim of my glass. Foo is a demon with cards when he decides to play seriously, and I would never think to match his skill in such a game, but even so his nature tends to get the better of him. When possessed of a winning hand his tail-tip flicks with expectation. It is a subtle clue to intended victory, and one only those who know him well can read. He eyed our guest sideways and blinked a slow R'rruthren blink. "You only play with me," he accused with a hint of tease, "because you know I will reveal if anyone is cheating with magic on the cards."

"Or pepper," Scarll pointed out. There was a moment's silence, and then the pair of them burst out laughing. I considered them both with studied patience while I reached to refill my glass.

"You were speaking of the King," I prompted, since Scarll seemed to have lost his earlier train of thought.

"Aye. Well, in that week of cold he left Nemithia garbed only as a Lion and rode north with a small escort of fellow knights. Reinwald left for Oscallon the day after, along with the Lady Deshart and her train of attendants."

He paused to take another sip from his goblet and dabbed fastidiously at his lips before continuing. "Rufus and I," he went on, "departed for Moderain by river boat, a great crowd of us making a proud show. The Prince went on to Towerstele castle and I –" he grinned. "I took a longer route to reach it.

"The meeting was an interesting event," he decided thoughtfully. "And the Duke arrived in style. He is ..." He considered his words carefully, " ... a very striking man."

"Did you meet him face to face?" Foo asked eagerly.

Scarll shook his head. "Not as such, no. I entertained certain associates of his, while Alwick and he kept conference under the Archmagus's hand. But I saw him, and I say to you, my lady, that he is not what you believe."

I frowned, uncertain of what he might mean. "I judge a man by his deeds, not his looks, my friend."

"I know. And Octian is a man of Carthery and all that that might imply. He is a shrewd politician, that much is sure. Alwick tells me he left thinking he had the best of the deal until he considered all of its ramifications. But there is something about the Duke that goes beyond mere intrigue. I cannot explain it exactly, but – I have met men who desired power, my lady. They cling to it with determination and arrogance, always wanting more. It becomes the most important thing in their lives. For Octian Desina I suspect it is merely a game that he plays – plays with relish and consummate skill, have no doubt of that, but still somehow a game."

I considered him thoughtfully, hearing the clear note of admiration in his words. The Merchant Princes of Daberon call life the Great Game, and many of them play it with relish. The Bargainer's contest is no simple game of fate and fortune, however – his strategies are far more complex than the turn of the Spinner's wheel, even if her hand is never entirely absent from them. It is a matter of wit and tactics, of bluff and bravado, hidden assets, and strategic retreat where necessary. It is because of it that Daberon itself has no need of central government, since each and every House weaves alliance and politics into even their simplest bargaining. Assets are measured by commitment and contract rather than mere possession, and Scarll is well schooled in that philosophy. Which made his admiration for the ruler of Carthery even more astonishing. The Velvet City has no word for honour in its vocabulary, betrayal and double dealing second nature within its walls. Loyalty belongs to the strong and cunning, those who fortune favours and who are generous with their rewards. Its politics and intrigues are a long way from the complex interweavings of the Merchant code and I said as much, watching for the man's reaction.

He laughed. "Not so far, my lady. Not so far at all. Just two sides of a coin, perhaps – or one a reflection of the other. You were right, that day in the garden. The Desinas have Merchant blood in their veins for certain, however dilute it may be elsewhere in the city. As for Octian himself – rumour has it a demon sired him, and I can see how such a tale began. He carries his presence like a cloak, and it belies his too pretty face and his seeming youth."

"I'd heard he was good looking, as men go," Foo remarked with a yawn that had more to do with the liquor than the conversation.

"Good looking?" Scarll chuckled softly. "The man is gorgeous. And slight, too – he is as slim and slender as a willow bound elfin, although there is no trace of season or forest colour in his skin or locks. He's as golden as his nickname, right down to the honey of his voice. Except for his eyes," the prince added with a thoughtful frown. "Those seem to have as many colours as the shift of the sea. Blue, green and grey." He shivered suddenly and reached for his glass to cover his discomfiture. "There is steel beneath the gold – steel, and power, too. Velvet wrapped, like his city. But Alwick tells me he is personable enough; just not a man to underestimate."

"A snowsnake has a pleasant demeanor until you step on its tail," I remarked mildly. "And I would trust the Duke of Carthery no further than I could carry the Athel Palace. Has he promised to keep his people in line?"

"As far as he is able, yes." Scarll grinned at my analogy. "The Legion are loyal enough; he recruits mercenaries rather than his own people and he pays them well. The Sansig honour him, too, which means the swamp-lands will pay lip service to the bargain if nothing else."

"All that accounts for," Foo pointed out, "is the border patrols, the deep swamp and the ships of the Desina line. What of the rest of it?"

Our visitor paused to stab at a tempting titbit with the point of his knife. "He was honest enough not to guarantee anything further. Alwick has offered to allow more grain and wool down the river if less poison comes up it, and the Duke will take the matter to Council accordingly. It may keep the lid on things for a while."

I sighed, putting down my empty goblet and staring into the fire. "Leaving Alwick free to concentrate on other matters, you mean."

"Ah." He threw me an admiring glance. "Then you have heard about the visit of the Kharad ambassador?"

Foo snorted. "She hears a lot of things. Many of them from you."

Scarll frowned at him, then chortled softly. "A point to you, whiskerbreath. I shall add it to your tally. Do not worry over much concerning the disturbance in the Iron Heights, my lady. Those in Highharren have too many internal concerns to snatch too strongly at their borders. The wounds are still raw from the last time they sought to extend their rule, and Kesiwik is too wracked with grief to look beyond her tower walls, let alone her country."

"Seven years," I wondered softly. "A long time to weep over the death of one consumed by your own sorcery."

"She loved her as her own," Scarll pointed out. "And could deny her nothing. Farance demanded to carry the witchfire. She was eaten by her own ambitions long before she succumbed to the flames."

"Better her than the whole of Asconar," Foo growled. "We'd have had stonefolk gnawing our bones for breakfast if she'd have had her way."

"Bad for business," the merchant decided firmly. "War, I mean. No profit on a battlefield."

"Scarll Scarlettini," I decided archly, "you are, without question, the most incorrigible rogue in the whole of Nemithia. Only you would assess the worth of war by its impact on profitability."

He was unperturbed by my affronted tone. "I, my House, and my countrymen, my lady. I can no more help my nature than you can, although I do not have the luxury of your Lady's hand to guide me."

"True enough," I sighed, letting the matter pass.

We drank a while longer and talked of inconsequential things before Scarll sought his leave and vanished into the night, the faithful Maris sheltering him from the worst of the wind. Foo curled up by the fire, mellowed by the warmth and the wine, and I left him to doze, dismissing Delph for what was left of the evening and seeking solitude in the highest chamber of my tower. Dispiriter lay quietly on the altar, candlelight reflected in her blade, and I ran my fingers along her length, stilling my heart and giving myself up to my Lady's presence.

It enfolded me softly, welcoming me with a touch that carried no urgency in it. Outside, the wind moaned with endless bitterness, the sound of my Lady weeping for her Son as he endures all the sufferings of mankind. I thought of Eachan, consumed by bitterness and jealousy, and of Reinwald, who had tried to help him and had only fuelled the flames. I thought of Kirby, watching his streets and his city, dedicated to holding back the tides of disorder and injustice. I thought of Alwick, carrying the needs of his people and defending his kingdom with words as well as steel. The wind howled a winter chorus, speaking of the sorrows of the world and taunting me with my own insignificance in the greater pattern of things. It was a bitter night, sharp with ice and the promise of winter yet to come.

I thought of Scarll, scurrying home through the darkened streets, and I had to smile.

Acknowledgements

The Known Kingdoms was originally devised as a potential campaign setting for Penelope Hill's University D&D group back in the late 1970s. At that point, the idea was to devise a variety of Kingdoms and principalities, along with a disparate group of religions, so that players could have varied backgrounds and various faiths, some conducive to co-operative play.

We should therefore acknowledge the initial input of the members of that group, who suggested ideas and commented on the Kingdom's early development. Chris, Kevin – and Damien, in particular, who helped shape a notable NPC, her holy sword and furry companion making her presence known, even at that early stage.

As it happens, nobody actually got to play in the Known Kingdoms – exams and other events got in the way. But the world went on bubbling and forming in the back of its creator's mind, and was there – fairly well defined, when the two of us started discussing what we might write together next.

We had met, not at University, but through the community of early UK Star Trek fandom. A slew of conventions, get-togethers, and very long phone calls cemented a firm friendship that has continued to the present day.

We'd already completed one collaborative novel, and thought we'd try something a little different. Parisan and the backdrop offered by the Known Kingdoms gave us the chance to tackle a self-contained mystery. Our heroine, familiar with her world and her city in particular, provided us with a perspective to work with. Stepping in the footsteps of Sherlock Holmes and his later counterparts, we would focus on the mystery and let the world unfold around the reader as our protagonists carried out their investigation.

We wrote it. We tried submitting it to a few publishers, but none of them wanted to consider it. So we put it aside and moved on to other things.

But we didn't forget about it, and thirty plus years later – thanks to Peter and Elsewhen Press, that story is now in print. The notes on the Known Kingdoms have grown richer and more detailed. There are more maps, many more notes on races and religions – and other characters, and other stories lurking in the 'to be written' pile.

So who else do we want thank? There are, of course, a whole slew of writers whose books, TV scripts, and graphic novels have inspired us over the years. For this book, the ones to note probably start with Gary Gygax, and buying the white box D&D set in a tiny backstreet games shop all those years ago. Then there is Ed Greenwood, creator of the Forgotten Realms, who showed us that a home built campaign can be rich and detailed enough to support the telling of tales as well as the fun of a dungeon crawl. Judith got her gaming experience from the City Lit group, in particular Simon, and from Jackie, as well as enjoying numerous games with Penny and her husband, Robin. The original 'gold box' games from SSI also deserve a mention – we played them together, and still find ourselves quoting lines from them. And no paladin-related story would be complete without a nod to Artix von Krieger. Thanks to Profantasy software and their Campaign Cartographer for assistance in creating our maps, and a grateful nod to Midjourney's bot for help in cooking up the cover image.

Finally, thanks to everybody who's listened to us talk about this story over the years. Despite the passage of time, we are still friends and we still use each other as beta readers. There may be more joint projects in the future – watch this space!

You can find us and information about our other projects at:

Welcome – The Known Kingdoms
(https://knownkingdoms.com/)

Judith's website
(jamortimore.com)

Elsewhen Press

delivering outstanding new talents in speculative fiction

Visit the Elsewhen Press website at elsewhen.press for the latest
information on all of our titles, authors and events; to read our blog;
find out where to buy our books and ebooks; or to place an order.

Sign up for the Elsewhen Press InFlight Newsletter at
elsewhen.press/newsletter

Also by Penelope Hill

Working Weekend

Penelope Hill

Sometimes authenticity sucks!

Marcus Holland, European Folklore expert and award-winning writer of Horror and Fantasy fiction, is guest of honour at the CoffinCon convention being held in an old gothic mansion-turned-hotel. He's looking forward to the weekend, as he's hoping for a break from the pressures of work, the enthusiasm of his agent and the demands of his ex-wife. There's to be a midnight masque, a Real Ale bar, and the convention committee have even arranged to have a 'real' vampire wandering the halls, to help add to the atmosphere.

From the moment Marcus arrives he starts to feel uneasy, but can't quite put his finger on the reason why. Although he soon comes to realise what is wrong, he knows he can't broadcast his concerns without being thought insane. Far from being a relaxing break he will be working harder than ever in order to safeguard his friends and fans.

ISBN: 9781911409717 (epub, kindle) / 9781911409618 (240pp paperback)

Visit bit.ly/WorkingWeekend

THE MAREK SERIES BY JULIET KEMP

1: THE DEEP AND SHINING DARK

A Locus Recommended Read in 2018

"A rich and memorable tale of political ambition, family and magic, set in an imagined city that feels as vibrant as the characters inhabiting it."   **Aliette de Bodard**
Nebula-award winning author of *The Tea Master and the Detective*

You know something's wrong when the cityangel turns up at your door
An agreement 300 years ago, between an angel and Marek's founding fathers, protects magic and political stability within the city. A recent plague wiped out most of the city's sorcerers. Reb, one of the survivors, realises that someone has deposed the cityangel without replacing it. Marcia, Heir to House Fereno, stumbles across that same truth. But it is just one part of a much more ambitious plan to seize control of Marek.

Meanwhile, city Council members connive and conspire, manipulated in a dangerous political game that threatens the peace and security of all the states around the Oval Sea. Reb, Marcia, the deposed cityangel, and Jonas, a Salina messenger, must work together to stop the impending disaster. They must discover who is behind it, and whom they can really trust.

ISBN: 9781911409342 (epub, kindle) / 9781911409243 (272pp paperback)
Visit bit.ly/DeepShiningDark

2: SHADOW AND STORM

"never short on adventure and intrigue... the characters are real, full of depth, and richly drawn, and you'll wish you had even more time with them by book's end. A fantastic read."   **Rivers Solomon**
Author of *An Unkindness of Ghosts*, Lambda, Tiptree and Locus finalist

Never trust a demon... or a Teren politician
The new Teren Lord Lieutenant has an agenda. A young Teren magician being sought by an unleashed demon, believes their only hope may be to escape to Marek where the cityangel can keep the demon at bay. Once again Reb, Cato, Jonas and Beckett must deal with a magical problem, while Marcia tackles a serious political challenge to Marek's future.

ISBN: 9781911409595 (epub, kindle) / 9781911409496 (336pp paperback)
Visit bit.ly/ShadowAndStorm

3: THE RISING FLOOD

"Fantasy politics with real nuance ... a fantastic read"   **Malka Older**
Author of the *Centenal Cycle* trilogy, Hugo Award Finalist

Hope alone cannot withstand a rising flood
A darkness writhes in the heart of Teren, unleashing demons on dissenters. Marek's five sorcerers with the cityangel can expel a single demon, but Teren has many. Storms rampage across the Oval Sea. Menaced by the distant capital, dissension from within, and even nature itself – will the rising flood lift all boats? Or will they be capsized?

ISBN: 9781911409984 (epub, kindle) / 9781911409885 (392pp paperback)
Visit bit.ly/TheRisingFlood

BY DAVID M ALLAN
QUAESTOR

When you're searching, you don't always find what you expect

In Carrhen some people have a magic power – they may be telekinetic, clairvoyant, stealthy, or able to manipulate the elements. Anarya is a Sponger, she can absorb and use anyone else's magic without them even being aware, but she has to keep it a secret as it provokes jealousy and hostility especially among those with no magic powers at all.

When Anarya sees Yisyena, a Sitrelker refugee, being assaulted by three drunken men, she helps her to escape. Anarya is trying to establish herself as an investigator, a quaestor, in the city of Carregis. Yisyena is a clairvoyant, a skill that would be a useful asset for a quaestor, so Anarya offers her a place to stay and suggests they become business partners. Before long they are also lovers.

But business is still hard to find, so when an opportunity arises to work for Count Graumedel who rules over the city, they can't afford to turn it down, even though the outcome may not be to their liking.

Soon they are embroiled in state secrets and the personal vendettas of a murdered champion, a cabal, a puppet king, and a false god looking for one who has defied him.

ISBN: 9781911409571 (epub, kindle) / 9781911409472 (304pp paperback)
Visit bit.ly/Quaestor-Allan

THIEVER

Change is not always as good as a rest

After the events in Jotuk at the end of *Quaestor*, Anarya is no longer a Sponger but is now a Thiever – when she takes someone's magic talent they lose it until she can no longer hold on to it. Worryingly, the power also brings a desperate hunger to take others' talents, just as the false god did. As Anarya struggles to control the compulsion, Yisul is fraught with worry and seeks help for her lover. But Jotuk is in upheaval; the Twenty-Three families are in disarray, divided over how the city should be governed.

In Carregis, the king seeks to establish himself as an effective ruler. First, though, he must work out whom he can trust.

Meanwhile, the priestesses of Quarenna and the priests of Huler are having disturbing dreams…

Thiever is the much anticipated sequel to David M Allan's *Quaestor*.

ISBN: 9781911409977 (epub, kindle) / 9781911409878 (386pp paperback)
Visit bit.ly/Thiever

SIMON KEWIN'S WITCHFINDER SERIES
"Think *Dirk Gently* meets *Good Omens*!"

THE EYE COLLECTORS
A STORY OF
HER MAJESTY'S OFFICE OF THE WITCHFINDER GENERAL
PROTECTING THE PUBLIC FROM THE UNNATURAL SINCE 1645

When Danesh Shahzan gets called to a crime scene, it's usually because the police suspect not just foul play but unnatural forces at play.

Danesh is an Acolyte in Her Majesty's Office of the Witchfinder General, a shadowy arm of the British government fighting supernatural threats to the realm. This time, he's been called in by Detective Inspector Nikola Zubrasky to investigate a murder in Cardiff. The victim had been placed inside a runic circle and their eyes carefully removed from their head. Danesh soon confirms that magical forces are at work. Concerned that there may be more victims to come, he and DI Zubrasky establish a wary collaboration as they each pursue the investigation within the constraints of their respective organisations. Soon Danesh learns that there may be much wider implications to what is taking place and that somehow he has an unexpected connection. He also realises something about himself that he can never admit to the people with whom he works…

ISBN: 9781911409748 (epub, kindle) / 9781911409649 (288pp paperback)
Visit bit.ly/TheEyeCollectors

THE SEVEN SUCCUBI
THE SECOND STORY OF
HER MAJESTY'S OFFICE OF THE WITCHFINDER GENERAL

Of all the denizens of the circles of Hell, perhaps none is more feared among those of a high-minded sensibility than the succubi.

The Assizes of Suffolk in the eighteenth century granted the Office of the Witchfinder General the power to employ 'demonic powers' so long as their use is 'reasonable' and 'made only to defeat some yet greater supernatural threat'. No attempt was made in the wording of the assizes to measure or grade such threats, however – making the question of whether it is acceptable to fight fire with fire a troublingly subjective one.

Now, in the twenty-first century, Danesh Shahzan, Acolyte in Her Majesty's Office of the Witchfinder General, had been struggling with that very question ever since the events of The Eye Collectors. An unexpected evening visit from his boss, the Crow, was alarming enough – but when it turned out to be to discuss his thesis on succubi, Danesh was surprised yet intrigued. Clearly, another investigation beckoned.

ISBN: 9781915304117 (epub, kindle) / 9781915304018 (334pp paperback)
Visit bit.ly/TheSevenSuccubi

You might also enjoy

Bookworm series by Christopher Nuttall

Bookworm

Elaine, an inexperienced witch in Golden City, has her life turned upside down when she triggers a magical trap to end up with all the knowledge in the Great Library stuffed inside her head. Avoiding the Inquisition she tries to understand what has happened to her. But she is a pawn in the dark plans of one who wants the Grand Sorcerer's power.

Bookworm won the Gold Award in the Adult Fiction category of the 2013 Wishing Shelf Independent Book Awards.

ISBN: 9781908168320 (epub, kindle) / 9781908168221 (368pp, paperback)

Visit bit.ly/Bookworm-Nuttall

Bookworm II – The Very Ugly Duckling

Not every ugly duckling becomes a swan ...

In the wake of the disastrous attack on the Golden City, Lady Light Spinner has become Grand Sorceress and Elaine, the Bookworm, has been settling into her positions as Head Librarian and Privy Councillor.   But any hope of vanishing into her books is negated when a new magician of staggering power appears in the city, one whose abilities seem to defy the known laws of magic.

ISBN: 9781908168382 (epub, kindle) / 9781908168283 (432pp, paperback)

Visit bit.ly/Bookworm2-Nuttall

Bookworm III – The Best Laid Plans

Elaine and Johan prepare to leave Golden City, with Daria and Cass, to search for the Witch-King. But Elaine is arrested on the orders of a new Emperor, puppet of the Witch-King. She must escape and destroy him. Privy Councillors and Heads of the Great Houses have bowed to the Emperor. Only Elaine and her friends can prevent an all-out war.

ISBN: 9781908168764 (epub, kindle) / 9781908168665 (400pp, paperback)

Visit bit.ly/Bookworm3

Bookworm IV – Full Circle

Until now the Witch-King had remained hidden as a lich. But Elaine was intent on his destruction. Bonded to the unknowingly powerful Johan, she was the only other magician who understood the deeper layers of magic. As they slowly made their way towards the catacombs in Ida where his lich was hiding, he had to rely on the new Emperor to stop them.

ISBN: 9781908168948 (epub, kindle) / 9781908168849 (416pp, paperback)

Visit bit.ly/Bookworm4

All now available as audiobooks from Tantor

About Penelope Hill

Penelope Hill has wanted to be a writer for as long as she can remember, and her fascination with both futuristic and fantastic worlds has fuelled that ambition ever since. She is an avid reader, a long time role-player and games-master, and loves world-building: designing exotic places, writing mythic histories, and crafting cultures. She's been a costumer and is busy developing her skills as a textile artist, so when she's not writing she can usually be found stitching, knitting, knotting, or exercising other creative skills. During her working life, she spent many years supporting services in local government, and eventually found herself contributing to the development of both local and national policy, particularly around privacy and confidentiality. The research for her PhD helped influence some of that work, but has also brought new perspectives to both her writing and her world building. While she has published academically, she prefers creative writing, and retirement has given her the opportunity to pursue her long standing ambition to become a professional author. She currently lives in Gloucestershire with five cats, a huge library of books, a treasure hoard of fabric and thread, and far too many dice.

About J. A. Mortimore

J A Mortimore (Judith) was born in London in 1953. She started writing stories at a young age and has never stopped. She wrote fanfiction for many years in a number of fandoms, all pre-internet. She has been active in science fiction and fantasy circles for longer than she cares to think about. She has a doctorate in policing young people. She has a short story in an anthology published in 2022 and has written space operas with romance which she plans to self-publish. Now retired, she lives in Gloucestershire with two friends, a number of cats, and far too many books and half-finished manuscripts.

Lightning Source UK Ltd.
Milton Keynes UK
UKHW010647171022
410608UK00002B/256

9 781915 304087